"The voices of Rutherford and Knox are woven into a historic tapestry of war, civil disobedience, justice, father's love, and family devotion. This boy of 60 found himself rooting for Angus!"

Robert Case, Director,
World Journalism Institute

"The narrative in *King's Arrow* has such a strong flow that the reader is carried along effortlessly. Not only is it an interesting story of serious and frightening true history, it involves the intellect of young people, and though *King's Arrow* may be for young fellows in particular, I intend to send a copy to my granddaughters, who, I am sure, will read it avidly."

Mrs. Robert G. Rayburn,
wife of the founder of Covenant College
and Theological Seminary

CROWN & COVENANT

Duncan's War, Book 1
King's Arrow, Book 2
Rebel's Keep, Book 3

KING'S ARROW

DOUGLAS BOND

ILLUSTRATED BY MATTHEW BIRD

Page design by Tobias Design
Typesetting by Michelle Feaster

Printed in the United States of America

Library of Congress Cataloging-in-Publication Data

Bond, Douglas, 1958-
King's arrow / Douglas Bond ; illustrated by Matthew Bird.
p. cm.— (Crown and covenant ; 2)
Sequel to: Duncan's War.
Summary: In Scotland in 1679, sixteen-year-old Angus M'Kethe and his family struggle to be true to their Covenanter faith as they face physical and religious persecution at the hands of King Charles II and his English and Highlander supporters.
ISBN 0-87552-743-4
[1. Covenanters—Fiction. 2. Christian life—Fiction. 3. Conduct of life—Fiction. 4. Presbyterian Church—Fiction. 5. Ayrshire (Scotland)—History—17th century—Fiction. 6. Scotland—History—1660–1688—Fiction. 7. Drumclog, Battle of, Scotland, 1679—Fiction.] I. Bird, Matthew, ill. II. Title.

PZ7.B63665Ki 2003
[Fic]—dc21

2003048614

For Brittany, Rhodri, Cedric, Desmond, and Giles

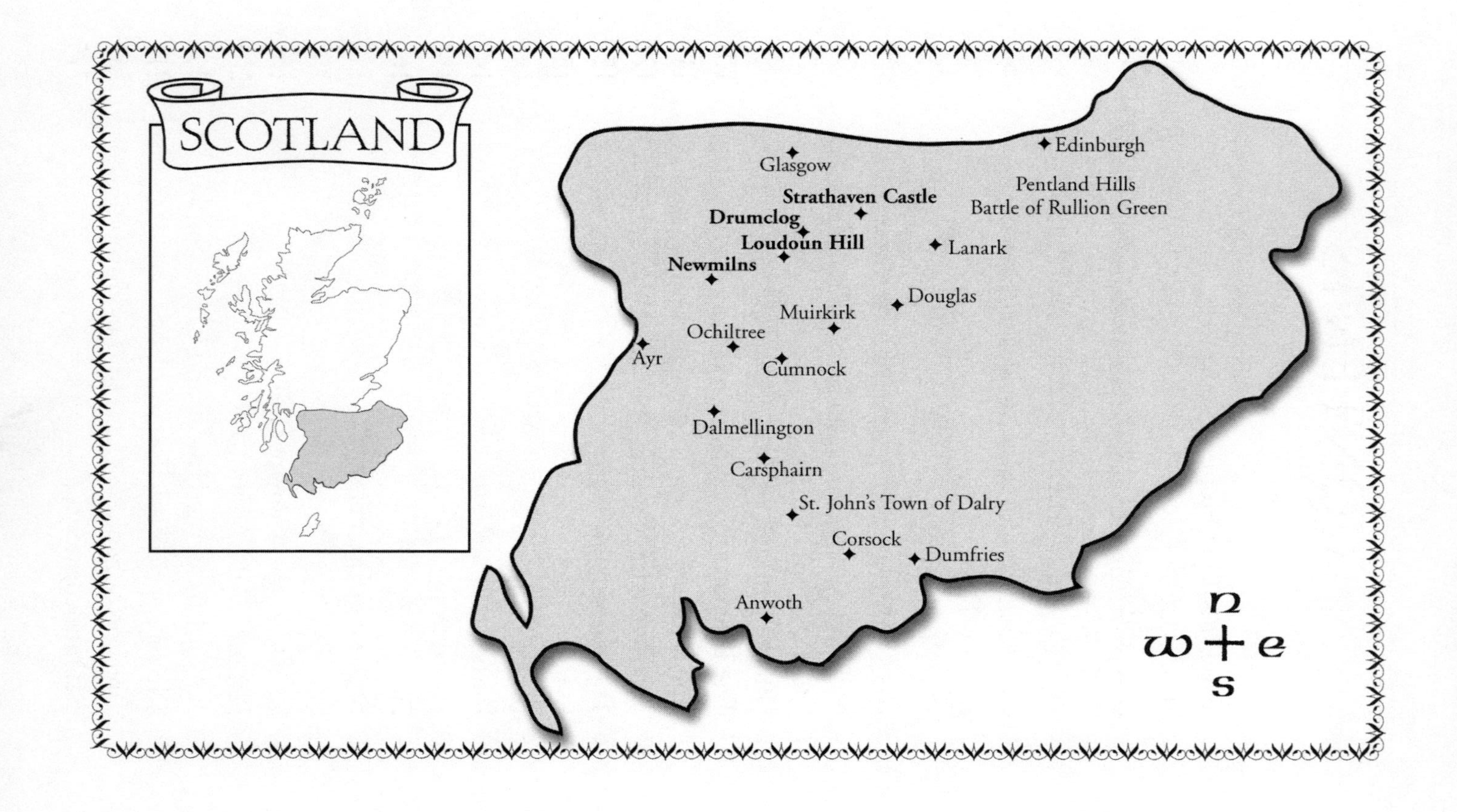
SCOTLAND
Glasgow
Edinburgh
Strathaven Castle
Pentland Hills
Battle of Rullion Green
Drumclog
Loudoun Hill
Lanark
Newmilns
Douglas
Muirkirk
Ochiltree
Ayr
Cumnock
Dalmellington
Carsphairn
St. John's Town of Dalry
Corsock
Dumfries
Anwoth
n
w
e
s

CONTENTS

"Grace withereth without adversity.

The devil is but God's master-fencer,

to teach us to handle our weapons."

Samuel Rutherford

1
TWO BIRDS, ONE STONE
(April 1679)

Angus M'Kethe lay on his back at the base of a bent tree, his sturdy legs crossed and stretched upward, resting against the gnarled trunk. The tree was an old sycamore tree, and its twisted branches seemed to be groping in all directions, as if frantic to hold its lonely place on the broad back of the wind-swept moor. In his hands Angus held the leather boards of a book, propped open on his broad chest, and his deep blue eyes raced hungrily down the page.

A handful of sheep, in a frenzy of gripping and tearing and gulping, cropped the spring moor grass nearby, and new lambs butted heads in the heather. At regular intervals, marked by the impatient turning of a page, the young man glanced at the sheep, and, when sure that all was well, resumed his reading.

Halfway down the next page, the plaintive bleating of a new lamb crept in on the story unfolding from the pages. Angus tore his eyes from the book and studied his little flock.

High moorland ewes delivered their lambs later in the spring than valley ewes, and just that morning Angus had helped Winnie, the oldest of their ewes, deliver up yet another healthy lamb—her thirteenth, one for every year of her adult life. Her lamb lay sleeping, looking like a tiny patch of late snow left in a hollow. Rising stiffly, Winnie waddled several yards and lapped the backwater of a nearby stream.

Angus reflected on how much his family was in debt to these timid creatures whose wool clothed them and whose meat, when they could afford it, nourished their bodies. One dark eyebrow raised, he glanced at the sky. It was a gray, drifting sort of day of broken light, but mostly shadows. Plenty of other creatures—anything from crows to wild Highlanders hired by the English to wreak havoc on Covenanting Lowland Scots—might be lurking nearby, ready to snatch one of his lambs. Angus's eyes narrowed into wary slits as he scanned the broad expanse of green and purple moorland and the hovering masses of gray and white slowly churning overhead.

Many an evening around the hearth had Angus listened eagerly as his father and brother told the story of his people's courage and faith when on every side their enemy descended with pillage, fire, and sword. They told of signing the National Covenant in 1638, wherein the faithful bound themselves with blood to uphold the Crown rights of the Redeemer in his Kirk. They told of the English Civil War and eventual betrayal by Parliament; of the restoration of the monarchy and the duplicity of Charles II; of the ejection of faithful ministers, fines, and executions; of their old life at Dalry in Galloway and of their friend and neighbor Ancient Grier; of the Pentland Rising; of the scathing defeat at Rullion Green in 1666; of more death. They told of his father's escape from execution and of hiding in the mines; of the brutal retaliation of Drummond and Daliel, who swept through Galloway like twin death angels. And they told of the fading strength of dear Ancient Grier, battered as he had been by the king's dragoons and beyond recovery, how the old man had breathed his last, and how, with tears, they had laid him to rest near the ruins of Dunfarg Castle. And, finally, they told of his family's flight to Ayrshire thirteen years ago.

And now daily reports unfolded of the unprincipled cruelties of James Turner's replacement, bloody John Graham of Claverhouse, a fanatical, armed high priest, commissioned to exterminate the enemies of the King. A gleeful Episcopal crusader, Claverhouse made it known that ridding Scotland of the gangrene of the Presbyterians, by shot and sword, by noose and boot, by rack and thumbscrew, by any means whatsoever, was his only ambition.

An involuntary shudder tingled down Angus's spine, and he rose onto one elbow and studied the moor closely. All looked peaceful—for the moment.

He returned to his book. It was a new book, published in England—just last year, 1678—and loaned to him by his friend, the good earl of Loudoun. With the restoration of Charles II, in 1660, came a sharp drop in the number of books published in Scotland, and the cost of the few available exceeded his imagination.

Angus couldn't exactly explain the quickening of his breath, the twitching of his eyes, and the gulping anticipation that he felt in his mind when he held a book in his hands. Books were like a devouring obsession to him. And this book—well, he'd never read a book like this one. Though written by an Englishman—no small obstacle for a Scot—he could not put it down.

"Aye, then, where was I?" he said aloud, his eyes running down the page. "Ah, here, then."

> . . . he espied a foul fiend coming over the field to meet him; his name is Apollyon. Now the monster was hideous to behold: he was clothed with scales like a fish, and they are his pride; he had wings like a dragon,

> feet like a bear, and out of his belly came fire and smoke; and his mouth was the mouth of a lion. When he was come up to Christian, he beheld him with a disdainful countenance, and thus began to question him.

Again the pitiful bleating of the new lamb broke in on the tale. But this time another sound caught his ear: the sassy cawing of crows.

"Foul fiends, all," he said under his breath.

In one fluid motion Angus closed the book, swung his legs down off the trunk of the tree, rolled over, and grabbed a yew bow strung and ready at his side. Silently, he stood, every muscle at full alert. He planted his feet, selected an arrow, and after wetting the feathers, he fitted the shaft onto the string.

To the average person crows might not seem like a shepherd's menace, but Angus knew better. He'd seen a mob of crows sweep down on a newborn lamb and, before the frantic ewe could clamber to its defense, peck out the eyes, and with their strong beaks, rip the helpless lamb open and fall to on the tender pulsing innards. And just this moment, three crows—black devils from hell—circled just above Winnie's newborn. He could run out waving his arms and shouting; that worked for a few minutes. But, though the crows were fully fifty yards away and in flight, Angus preferred his bow. What good was a claymore from this distance? No, Angus had come to prefer the bow to any other weapon. To him, there was no other weapon.

Eyeing the plunging and dipping flight of the crows, he waited. Then with a flash of sunlight as it twisted its wings, one of the greedy birds dived steadily toward the lamb. Angus drew the string and raised his bow. Squinting down the shaft, he calculated wind speed and, from long practice, the trajectory of his arrow—and let fly.

His aim was true, and the arrow passed cleanly through the crow's body. It fell lifeless to the ground. Lingering for a moment, a single black feather hovered in the air—and then floated gently to the ground.

No sooner had the arrow left the string, and Angus fitted another and readied himself. The two remaining crows faltered.

"Not sure what ye're about, are ye?" said Angus under his breath. If they looked the situation over and decided to fly away to easier pickings elsewhere, Angus was reasonably confident he could bring one more of them down as they retreated. Scowling, he brushed a strand of dark, peat-colored hair from his eyes. The pair circled warily. Then they turned as if to fly away.

For an instant, Angus hesitated; after all, they were leaving.

Then that pitiful bleating of his newborn lamb broke in on his concentration. His eyes narrowed, and like a flash, Angus drew, aimed, and shot.

Time slowed to a crawl as he watched the flight of his arrow. His shot was true. He nodded with satisfaction as his arrow passed cleanly through the nearest bird. But what was this? At precisely the same instant, the second bird came in line with the first. And as the first bird dropped, his same arrow passed with a shudder through the left wing of the second crow. The first bird died in flight. The second screeched and veered sharply left. Then, amidst flying feathers and contortions of wings and body, it tumbled into the heather.

As Angus strode toward where the bird had fallen, he saw a black flurry rise from the heather and drop again. The bird was still alive and frantic to get away. A sudden twinge of remorse arose in Angus's mind. He slowed his pace. They *were* turning to fly away, he mused. Should he have let them go? But crows are crows, aren't they? He thought he knew the answer. His pace slowed further.

Two years ago Angus had shot his first crow in flight just as the bird was about to land in a beech tree. He had swelled with delight as it fell to the ground: he'd been trying to hit one for years. Then he spotted the nest. With dread rising in his heart, he climbed the tree. When he reached it, a single baby crow, expecting to see its mother, flinched in horror as it stared at Angus's broad face. Then it opened its pathetic little beak expectantly. Angus had nothing to give it. Thereafter, almost as if performing an act of penance, he doted on the little bird. He was not entirely sure why. He'd always thought he hated crows—lamb killers, they were. But he even gave this one a name, Flinch. And when the raven-hued bird was strong enough, he put it in the family dovecote with the pigeons. Maybe they would have a good influence on the crow.

Now, after two years, Angus rarely even thought of Flinch as a crow. The bird had seemed to develop more of the gentle manners of a pigeon than the harsh ones of a crow—well, more or less. Angus had to smile as he thought of the now full-grown coarse black bird perched alongside the gentle pigeons, their soft cooing broken at intervals by its jolting, raucous caws. Angus did wonder what he would do with Flinch. It couldn't carry important messages as he hoped one day to teach the pigeons to do. What good are crows, anyway? Sure, they clean up after the dead. He'd been reading about birds in another book the earl had lent him, and for some time now, he'd been talking to Flinch in hopes that the bird might eventually mimic his voice and talk. But so far, it just clicked and cawed nonsensically back at him—like any other crow.

His steps heavy, Angus neared the fallen bird. With a desperate beating of its good wing, the creature made a pitiful lunge upward, only to fall exhausted on the moor. Angus drew closer. Its wing and side glistened oily black with blood, and feathers littered the ground all around it. Again he thought of Flinch.

"I'd hadnae quarrel wi' ye," Angus said aloud, "if ye'd left my lamb alone. Ye've gone and brought this on yer own self. And if I left ye to mend . . ." His voice trailed off. It would come back after his lambs, that much was sure.

Part of him felt miserable. He knew this crow would die. An angry flush rose on his cheeks, but he couldn't make out if he was angry at the crow, at himself, or at something more.

Then he reached down and lifted a large stone. Weighing it pensively in his hands, Angus glanced back at where Winnie nuzzled her lamb. Oblivious to the treachery it had just escaped, the lamb waggled its wooly tail with contentment.

His teeth clenched, Angus turned, raised the stone with both hands, and held it poised over the dying crow.

2
HOW LONG?

Angus paused at the brim of the moor and gazed out over the rich green valley that spread out below. Sweet smells of meadow grass, heather blossoms, and the earthy aromas of sheep and cattle mingled pleasantly in the cool evening air. Angus drew in a deep breath, and the furrows that for several minutes had clouded his brow softened. Slinging his bow over his shoulder, he took from a leather shoulder bag a roll of paper. With a stick of charcoal, he wrote for several moments, pausing often and tapping on his forehead. Sheep and lambs mulled about his legs.

The muscles of his face seemed to relax as he watched the reds and purples of the setting sun play along the steep western slope of Loudoun Hill, rising like a waking giant from the valley below. Peat smoke curled into the scene from the evening fires in the village of Darvel, and farther to the west, from Newmilns, the tang of the peat reek mingled faintly with the cool evening air. His eyes followed the silvery path of the River Irvine westward, where just visible at the base of the hill stood the turrets and battlements of Loudoun Castle, the home of the kindly earl of Loudoun and his lady. He scribbled something more on his roll of paper, then carefully tucked it away in his pouch. Not for the first time, he unknowingly wore a coal black finger smudge on his brow, with a streak running down each cheek.

From high atop the whaleback of the moor, he could just pick out the two clusters of cottages that made up what was left of the villages. A frown returned to his face. Last winter, the winter of 1678, Lauderdale and the Privy Council, with the full approval of the diabolical Archbishop Sharp, unleashed eight thousand wild Highland men on Ayrshire. They descended like fiends above the law, and encouraged by zealous Claverhouse, they turned the once peaceful valley into a place of fear and hunger. The English king's government in Edinburgh turned a blind eye to all injustice—toward Covenanters. Houses were burned and sheep and cattle were devoured, men who resisted were thrown in prison, some were shot in full view of their families—a favorite method of bloodthirsty Claverhouse. As food ran low and cattle were carried off, tensions among those faithful to the Covenant mounted daily. Thirteen years had passed, and men again talked of armed resistance—of war.

"Home, then," Angus called to his scattering flock.

Moments later he led his little band of sheep through a narrow cut in the moor that opened into a cluster of three low stone cottages, their deep thatched roofs blending with the moor grass and heather. Lowland hills and valleys were sparsely settled with many such ferm-touns, small farms clustered together for mutual support—and defense.

"Lend a hand, brother," called a man's voice.

Angus looked up. Leaning into the steepness of the roof, a man in his later twenties with hair the color of sunrise before a stormy day grinned down at Angus.

"Toss up that sheaf of thatch, then," the man called.

Angus pulled his bow over his head and set it down with his arrows and pouch.

"Aye, I'll be throwing of it," he called up with a grin, "if, Duncan, ye can be catching of it."

With that he picked up the bundle of heather and gave it a heave.

"If I can be catching of it," mumbled Duncan, with a snort, as he lashed the bundle of heather in place. With a shearing clipper, he trimmed the stray ends of heather. Then he stepped nimbly down the crow steps of the gable and jumped the final few feet to the ground. From where it lay waiting, a black-and-white border collie rose stiffly to its feet, and, with a quiver in its hindquarters and a tremulous shake of its hind leg, made its way to where Duncan landed.

"Are ye all right, then, Paton?" Duncan asked as he gently stroked the dog's black muzzle, flecked now with gray. "Ye're a good old thing, that ye are."

Angus liked Paton, but he knew that as far as Paton was concerned, there was no one else in all the world except Duncan. As the dog had grown older, its loyalty had become even more firmly defined. Angus respected this.

"Och, then, that's done," said Duncan, looking back at the roof.

"Aye, it is," said Angus.

"Did ye see anything while ye were lounging around up on the moor?" asked Duncan, nodding upward. Then, with a grin, he added, "And did ye drive away all the oppressors of the Kirk with yer bow?"

"I saw nothing on the moor but heather," replied Angus levelly. "But as to my driving them off with my bow; I'd rather be armed with it any day over yer musket."

"Would ye, then?" said his brother.

"Aye," Angus said firmly.

His brother laughed.

"Well, now it's time for ye to do a bit of real work," said Duncan good-naturedly. "I ken ye've been up on the moor shooting yer bow—or reading one of the earl's books. Or maybe ye've been playacting that ye're a savage Indian from those American colonies—ye've got the war paint on yer forehead and cheeks again."

Angus reddened as he scrubbed at his face.

"Well, lad, as I say, now it's time for real work," continued Duncan, signaling his brother to follow.

"Ye judge me," said Angus, grinning, "by how *ye* used to look after sheep."

Duncan took a playful jab at his younger brother as they strode over to where someone had been piling stones in what appeared to be a growing wall of defense.

"Do I, then?" replied Duncan. "Leastwise, I never smudged up my face while tending the flock."

"Not the account Mother renders," said Angus.

"Och. Now, then, fall to. Father wants this wall finished."

Shoulder to shoulder, the brothers bent to the work of laying stones in the wall. Though Duncan stood several inches taller, Angus, broader at the shoulders, and with arms and hands that seemed almost too big for his body, carried himself in a manner that made him appear strong, deliberate, and grown up beyond his years.

"Word is," said Duncan, growing more sober, "the Highlander barbarians have quartered themselves on the Hamiltons."

"How many?" asked Angus, grunting as he hefted a large stone.

"Enough, so I heard, that what's left of their oats the brutes will devour in less than a fortnight."

"Then blithely on to the next family," said Angus.

"Aye," said Duncan, smashing a stone onto the pile, "unless they be stopped."

"Wait, Duncan," said Angus. "When they're finished stealing all from the Hamiltons, ye don't suppose they'd prey on old folks, then?"

"The Whytes live only a stone's throw from the Hamiltons," said Duncan. "I don't suppose they'd scruple about their age. They want anything of value, and they don't much care from whom they take it."

Angus bit his lower lip at the thought that formed in his mind.

"Ye're thinking of the lad," said Duncan, studying his brother's face.

"Aye," said Angus, frowning. "Willy's not like other folk, ye ken that, Duncan."

Angus felt the heat rising in his face, but it was not from the strain of lifting the heavy stones. Some people referred to Willy as a half-wit—Half-wit Willy—they'd say, but Angus, ordinarily not easily ruffled, would find himself breathing hard and clenching his teeth and fists when folks called him that. Though he'd learned a deep reluctance for killing from his father, if an English dragoon or a Highlander tried to hurt the Whytes—especially Willy—Angus would do whatever necessary to protect the family.

"Will there be another rising?" Angus said the words deliberately.

Duncan cleared his throat. "I were just nigh on yer age, Angus," he said, hefting a large stone in place on the defense work, "when all Galloway rose in defense of justice and the Kirk."

"Nay, Duncan," said Angus, looking around for a slightly larger stone than his brother's. "Ye had but fourteen years in 1666. I can do my numbers."

"But ye had only three years, then," said Duncan with a grin.

"Aye, and ye had only fourteen."

"But having but three years, Angus," said his brother, "what do ye ken of those days?"

"I ken how to do my numbers," said Angus. "The year of our Lord, 1666 to right now, the year of our Lord, 1679, is but thirteen years. I can cipher that much, Duncan. And that makes me to be having sixteen years and not yer fourteen years."

"Aye, but ye're forgetting that I too have thirteen years added to my fourteen years, and, thus, older and—"

"—and wiser," added Angus, tossing a clod of earth at his brother. "Don't ye forget the wiser bit."

"Aye, and wiser," Duncan nodded slowly. "And all that being true, ye're obliged to be giving me a sight more respect that this lot."

"Hail, Duncan," said Angus, dropping to one knee.

"Och, then," said Duncan. "Leave off, or I'll make ye part of the wall."

"So Master Duncan," continued Angus, "how many did ye slay in 1666 at the Green?"

The stone Duncan held in his hand fell to the sod with a *wump,* and he turned almost fiercely on his brother. "What do ye ken of the battle of Rullion Green," he said slowly, his voice now listless and detached as if Angus were no longer there. Duncan fell silent and gazed off down the valley, a rumpled lock of red hair twirled in the evening breeze.

Angus frowned. He'd seen this reaction from his brother before, and it puzzled him.

"Duncan, tell me—"

"Och, Angus," broke in Duncan, his eyes flashing at his brother. "Ye've never been at hand when real battle's joined, when real musket lead's flying about. And when the last roar of musket has sounded, and the last bloody sword is put up, ye've never walked the battlefield strewn with the twisted bodies of the dead and dying, hearing their groans and seeing the sod soaked red with their blood."

Angus stared back at his brother. It was all true. He'd only heard about these things; he'd never seen them with his own eyes.

"Aye," continued Duncan, passing his hand across his forehead. "Angus, what do ye ken of such things? Ye were holed up in the mines with the womenfolk whittling arrows. Come to think of it, wee brother"—he nodded at Angus's bow and arrows propped against the wall—"not much has changed."

"Ye're right, then," said Angus, heaving a sigh.

"Aye, that I am," agreed Duncan, looking suspiciously at his brother.

The spell was broken and Angus tried grinning at his brother.

"Ye don't think much of bows and arrows," said Angus casually.

"Aye, that I don't," agreed Duncan.

"Well, then, I challenge ye—to a duel," said Angus, mock seriousness in his tone. "Ye choose yer weapon. I'll choose mine."

"A duel?" said Duncan. "*Ye*, a duel with *me?*"

"They'll be no dueling in my household," their father broke in, dropping a wooden wheelbarrow on its pegs with a thump. Duncan and Angus scrambled to set another stone in place on the wall. Then they turned to help their father.

"I'll do that," said Angus, reaching for the handles of the wheelbarrow.

"Old I'm growing, that's true," said his father, a smile rising from beneath his red beard, now flecked with gray, and spreading across his weathered features. "But while strength remains," grunting, he upended the load, and rocks clattered into a pile near the wall, "I intend to use it."

He wiped his brow, but in midstroke he frowned at the unfinished wall. "Och, then. Has *yer* strength failed ye, lads?" He put his big hands on Angus's shoulders, then gave his son's biceps a squeeze. "Aye, so I thought. There's strength and to spare in those limbs." Again the big man eyed the wall. "But it looks as if yer strength went all into talking more than working this while."

"We're sorry, Father," said Angus, grabbing up a large stone.

"Father, yer son Angus, here," said Duncan, setting another stone in place, "has challenged me to a duel."

"I heard," said their father. "A duel, Angus?"

"Not the killing kind, Father," explained Angus, hastily. "At a target. Duncan with his musket a-rumbling and coughing and smoking away, and me with my bow and arrows. Not that there's ever much killing at duels even when men are actually aiming pistols at each other. I read somewhere that, aim ever so careful as ye may, ye've only one chance in eight of even hitting yer man in a duel; only one chance in fourteen of killing him. Nevertheless, I'll settle for target shooting."

"Ye ken Duncan's a fair shot with a musket?" said their father.

"I'd not want to test my bow against lesser," said Angus.

Sandy M'Kethe eyed his sons. He too had been curious at all Angus insisted about his bow. From when his son could first toddle about, Angus had devoured all the old stories about the superiority of the longbow in ancient wars. And Angus often spoke about how as recently as thirty years ago in the English Civil War some of the Scots preferred fighting with the longbow.

A grin spread across Duncan's face as he watched his father's features.

"Name yer target, then," said Sandy M'Kethe.

"Crows," said Angus, "in flight. Three shots each. Whoever brings down the most wins."

"Nay, but ye'd have the advantage of not scaring them off with the noise of yer first shot," protested Duncan, scowling.

"Aye, and now ye've gone and switched to my arguments," said Angus. "And I might add, reloading tends to go a sight faster with the bow. Are ye sure ye want to be doing this, Duncan?"

"Aye, I'll do it," growled Duncan, but he ran his hand nervously through his red hair as he spoke. "But we shoot at a fixed target from, say—fifty yards."

"Agreed," said Angus, grinning slyly. "Only fifty yards, did ye say?"

"But they'll be no shooting foolishness," said their father, " 'til I say so and until this portion of the wall's secure. With all yer noisemaking, we'll need all the defense we can muster against Claverhouse and plundering Highlanders come to investigate the shooting."

"Aye, another point for the bow," said Angus, rolling a large stone to the base of the wall. "Lend a hand with this one, Duncan."

Duncan snorted as he helped lift the stone in place.

3 KING AND KIRK

Squawk!" called Flinch next morning as Angus lifted him up onto his shoulder. The large black bird ran its beak through Angus's hair and nibbled at his ear. Brushing its beak aside gently, Angus offered it a kernel of corn.

"Angus, ye go along with yer mother and sister," said Sandy M'Kethe, "and tend to the needs of the Whytes." He looked at the darkening clouds and frowned. "Keep a keen eye out for Highlanders. Though they seldom venture out too early in the morning, ye're best to take along yer bow—for a walking stick, that is."

"Aye, Father."

"The Whytes are so frail," said Angus's sister Jennie. "Sometimes I wonder just how they continue to live through it all."

"If the English-loving tyrants had their way," snapped Mary M'Kethe, Angus's mother, as she arranged in a basket two thick pairs of wool socks she'd just finished knitting for the old couple, "there'd be none of us, mark ye, living through any of this plundering and pillaging. I hate the thought that our wool and my socks might be warming the foul-smelling toes of some thieving Highlander."

"It would be a pity," said Sandy M'Kethe, "but make no mistake, King Jesus rules Highlanders. He even rules the likes of bloody Claverhouse. Come what may, our Redeemer's still on his throne."

"Aye, but that foul fiend Charles of England," said Mary, "does all he can to make off with it and set his own self on it above the Kirk. I'll have none of it."

"And nor shall I," agreed her husband. "But we are bound by Holy Scripture to render honor to the king."

"But only in matters civil and political," added Jennie with a persuasive lilt to her tone, her blue eyes wide and intense. "Render to Caesar the things that are Caesar's, and to God the things that are God's. So it says in the Holy Book."

Angus nodded in agreement. Thirteen years had turned Jennie into a young woman, and since Duncan and Fiona now had families of their own, Angus and Jennie had grown to see each other not merely as childhood playmates, but as the closest of friends and confidants. Moreover, Jennie's flights of temper and meanness had almost entirely disappeared, and under the careful nurture of her pious mother and father, she had developed a firmness of faith and a clarity of affection that Angus saw as a sort of noble good sense. He overheard his father and mother refer to it as wisdom. Either way, Jennie had it, and Angus loved his sister for it. He watched as Jennie brushed aside a wavy lock of auburn hair from her face.

There was another thing about Jennie, mused Angus. For some time now, it had crept up on him, though he did his best to ignore it, but Jennie had, well, rather suddenly become very pretty—for a girl, that is. Prettier than any girl he'd ever seen—next to his mother, of course.

"Aye, Jennie," replied her father. "But it's the sorting out which is God's and which is Caesar's—that's where things get all squally."

"Seems to me," said Angus, "that King Charles fancies it's all his."

"When in fact," agreed Jennie, "all things are God's."

"Aye, but ye cannae deny," said their father, "that sinners that we are, we must have civil government."

"Aye, to uphold the Law of God," said Angus.

"And for keeping justice in the land," added Jennie.

"But I cannae see," continued Angus, "that the king giving bloody license to John Graham of Claverhouse—license to kill the innocent—how there's any justice in that."

"Aye, I heard tell from dear Morag that he calls himself," said Mary M'Kethe, "'the terror of the godly.' What kind of king, says I to Morag, hires a man that makes that kind of boast?"

"True enough," agreed Sandy M'Kethe. "Claverhouse makes Turner look like a schoolboy."

"So, what when Caesar resorts to lying and breaking covenant with his subjects, what then?" asked Mary M'Kethe, tucking a strand of russet hair streaked with gray behind her ear, a flush rising in her cheeks. She turned and added Crowdie cheese and two golden loaves of bread to the basket.

"For one thing," said Sandy M'Kethe, "we cling more faithfully to the other King. And finding our hope more and more in his Kingdom, we gain strength to endure the base tyranny of this manmade one. Troubles though there be on every hand, we hope in God our King, the sure and certain refuge for his Kirk."

"King and Kirk! King and Kirk!" screeched Flinch suddenly, proudly strutting back and forth on Angus's shoulder.

"What's this!" cried Angus's mother.

"Ye've gone and done it, Angus!" said Jennie, laughing and clapping her hands with delight.

"King and Kirk! King and Kirk!" said the bird again.

"Nae, 'twas Father's words what done it," said Angus, a

broad grin breaking across his face. He stroked Flinch's beak and head as he spoke.

"Och, we've all heard ye these weeks," replied his father, "repeating 'King and Kirk' in its raven ears."

"King and Kirk!" screeched Flinch again.

"He likes the attention," laughed Angus.

"I'd never hae believed it," said his mother, "save for hearing of it wi' my own ears."

"How'd ye manage to do it, Angus?" asked his father.

"Well, the idea for trying it came," said Angus, "while I was reading one of the earl's books."

"Aye, it would be that," said his father, smiling.

Four years ago, prompted by his son's hunger for learning, Sandy M'Kethe sought the council of the fugitive ministers Mr. King, Mr. Welsh, great-grandson of John Knox and the minister who had prayed with James Turner years ago during the Pentland Rising, and the more militant minister Mr. Douglas. Under the tyranny of the monarch and his minions, books and learning were hard to come by, and the universities at Glasgow, Edinburgh, St. Andrew's, and Aberdeen had become centers of episcopal propaganda, dangerous places for the sons of Covenanters. After lengthy conversation with the earl, Angus had begun pursuing what amounted to a private tutorial, reading under the careful scrutiny of the good earl. Angus's interests ranged widely, and the more he read, the more he wanted to read.

"I hae one clever brother," Jennie laughed, stroking the big bird. "All those hours ye spent talking at the creature—we feared ye'd gang daft—and now this."

"Can he say anything else?" asked his father.

"Alas, that's all his stock and store," explained Angus, tapping the bird's beak. "The bird can say but nothing more."

"There my baby Angus goes a-rhyming again," said his mother, ruffling his hair and planting a kiss on his cheek as she said it.

4 WILLY WHYTE

"Isn't it lovely?" said Jennie, halting. She smiled as the sunlight shone on the red sandstone cottages just coming into view through the trees.

Angus looked at his sister before answering. It was a pretty village huddled in the Irvine valley; *was*, that is, before the king's Commissioner Lauderdale and Archbishop Sharp, vulgar worldlings both, turned the brutish Highlanders loose in an effort to destroy Presbyterian worship and force the Covenanters in the region to submit to the king as head of the Church.

"If only the lackeys of King Charles," said Angus, his eyes darting warily from side to side, "would leave these poor folks be, then it would be lovely."

"Aye," said Jennie with a sigh.

"Did ye ken, Jennie, that savage Claverhouse rides a black charger that answers to the name—*Satan*? Did ye ken this?"

"He rides a horse called *Satan*?" said Jennie, a disbelieving lilt in her voice. "Who told ye this?"

"William Cleland. He kens these things."

"What kind of man would name his horse—*Satan*?" said Jennie in wonder.

Newmilns Village

Carrying the basket of food between them, Angus and Jennie had descended the moor and now followed the River Irvine westward. Through the trees they saw a beltie cow with its white-on-black calf standing in the river inhaling a drink of cool water. The cow raised its great black head, and a deep, gurgling lowing mingled with the surrounding village sounds: yapping dogs, clattering wheels, scolding mothers, the squeals and scuffling of children, and the throaty murmuring of chickens.

The stout sandstone tower of Loudoun Keep rose above the sparse cottages that made up what remained of the village of Newmilns, and gulls perched in formation along the crow-stepped gables of the new Loudoun Parish Kirk, as if waiting to prey on a dumping ground. The old kirk near the castle fell out of use in 1633 when local men built the present building situated more near the center of the once growing village.

"Why doesnae someone take them down?" asked Jennie, her face pale as she gazed at the fixed pikes near the village square.

Angus followed her gaze. The grizzled remains of several heads and gnarled hands, their fingers grasping at the air, were spitted atop the pikes. One of those heads had been there for thirteen years.

"Donnae look on them, Jennie."

"Duncan tells of one of them," his sister went on. "One of those heads is the head of Matthew Paton, the kindly shoemaker, Duncan's friend at Rullion Green."

"Aye, it is so," said Angus.

"But why hasnae someone given them a proper burial?"

"The king forbids it," said Angus, feeling his anger rising. "He wants them left as a grim reminder of what happens to any and all who resist his 'divine right.' Now, turn away, Jennie, and come along."

Moments later, Angus and Jennie drew near the old stone bridge. They heard a steady rubbing, broken by a watery swish and slap, coming from the river near the bridge. An old woman squatted on the bank, her thin white hair floating on the breeze, a meager pile of laundry at her side.

Few in Newmilns, though fiercely loyal to the faith of the "Thundering Scot," John Knox, and determined to keep the Sabbath, few ever darkened the doors of that once-beloved village church. Meanwhile, fines for nonattendance grew heavier by the week. After faithful Mr. John Nevay was ousted from Loudoun pulpit in 1662, a succession of bishop's men came and went. The latest slurred and stumbled his way through the hated liturgy of William Laud, and it was well known that he spent much more time drinking and carousing than praying and preaching.

"I only wish those walls rang," said Angus, looking back down the narrow street at the church building, "with the preaching of Mr. King. He's like Father."

"How so is he?" asked Jennie.

Angus narrowed his eyes and frowned in thought before replying.

"His preaching's strong—like Father is. And his preaching's somehow . . . well—"

"Gentle?" said Jennie.

"Aye, that'd be it, gentle," said Angus.

"Like Father is," said Jennie.

"Aye. But I donnae ken exactly how those things go together."

"And Mr. John Welsh," continued Jennie, "he too preaches with a thundering strength, like his great-grandfather Mr. Knox—so I'm told."

"Aye, and with a gentleness," said Angus, "that makes ye weep to believe what he says—no matter what the latest punishment is for believing of it."

"Aye," agreed Jennie with a shudder. She'd heard the reports of how the king's henchmen treated Covenanter ministers when they caught them preaching. "They take great risks, Angus, and all on our behalf."

"That they do," said Angus. "Aye. But I think King Charles finds it difficult"—he picked up a rock and hurled it with a *kerplunk* into the river—"to force those in Scotland who really do believe to submit to the mob of bishops and buffoons—who do not believe."

"And may he find it impossible," said Jennie, "and just give up."

"Aye, may he. But I just hope," said Angus, "that there'll be some of us left when he does."

They neared the old woman. Her thin white hair caught the light as she tilted her head from side to side, fondly intent on her work as if just now nothing else mattered so much as purging that last impurity from her family's clothes. Oblivious to their approach, her bony hands, twisted and stiff with age, coaxed the dirt from a much-mended pair of trousers.

"Good morning to ye," called Angus.

Her scrubbing didn't stop, nor did she look up.

"She'll not be hearing ye," said Jennie, "unless ye call louder than that. She's near deaf, ye ken that."

"Aye," said Angus.

"Aaangus!" an excited voice squealed from the tall grass just up the bank.

"Aaangus M'Kethe! My bonny, bonny friend Aaangus!"

Though the old woman had not heard Angus's voice, Willy had. Willy was full-grown and old enough that his once autumn-brown hair was now the color of sand. But for some reason, Willy had never stopped being a child. And now, like a child, with arms spread wide and with a smile of innocent delight breaking across his features, he rushed at Angus.

Angus smiled and set down the basket and braced his feet for the impact.

Though long ago his mind had decided it liked being eight years old so much it would just stay eight, Willy had never really figured out that his body was full-grown and heavy.

"Stand clear, Jennie," said Angus softly as Willy lumbered closer.

The bone-jarring impact now received, Angus patted his friend on the fleshy shoulders. For the next several moments Willy was too overcome with excitement for Angus or Jennie to decipher much of what he said. The old woman, Willy's mother, looked on and smiled. Meanwhile, a labored scraping and tapping came from the dark opening of the cottage, and old David Whyte emerged from the shadows leaning heavily on a rustic cane—one in each hand. He halted, blinked confusedly in the sunlight, and cupped a broad hand around his ear, trying to make out the cause of his son's excitement. At last, a flash of recognition came to his eyes, and a smile tugged at the deep, weathered trenches of his face.

"Ye've gone and brought yer black crow with ye," said Willy, clutching his hands together as he caught sight of the bird. The boy in a man's body extended a hand cautiously toward Flinch.

"Steady, then," said Angus under his breath to his crow.

After reaching and pulling back several times, each time with a giggle and a "Dare I touch 'im? Dare I?" Willy finally set his big hands clumsily on Flinch's head.

But at just that moment, the crow decided to show off its new vocabulary.

"King and Kirk!" it screeched.

Willy yanked his hand away and nearly fell backwards with the effort. At the same instant, he screamed like a terrified child.

Flinch flapped its wings and cawed, climbing rapidly from Angus's shoulder to the top of his head and back again.

"Aye, then, Willy," said Angus in a soothing tone. "Ye've nothing to fear from old Flinch. Nothing at all to fear."

"Aye, Willy," added Jennie. "He's just an old bird. And he'll not be hurting ye."

"He talked," said Willy, staring warily at the crow.

"Aye," agreed Angus.

"How'd he do it?" asked Willy, yanking at his hair with both hands and blinking rapidly in bewilderment.

"I read somewhere that some birds, crows included," explained Angus, "can be taught to speak."

"Animals cannae talk," said Willy, grinning. "They cannae, can they?" He smiled at Angus for reassurance.

"Well, not like ye and I can speak," agreed Angus. "That is, they can't think . . . well, like ye and I think, Willy."

Willy nodded his head vigorously. "I ken that."

"King and Kirk! King and Kirk!" screeched Flinch, as if to prove them wrong.

Willy frowned. Suddenly, he sprang to one side of Angus and crouched low, peering suspiciously behind him. When he saw no one, he looked sideways at Jennie, and blinking even more rapidly than before, he ran first one hand then the other through his hair. Angus detected a tremor in his friend's hands as the man clenched at his hair. Then, Willy brightened, as if an idea suddenly occurred to him.

"Wait," he called, then with a laugh he then turned and lumbered into the cottage. Jennie and Angus looked helplessly at each other. A moment later Willy returned with the family cat.

Holding it at arm's length, the cat's tail twitching in irritation, Willy said, "Teach Puss."

"Teach him what?" asked Angus.

"To talk," insisted Willy, a hint of irritation in his tone.

"I cannae do it," laughed Angus.

"I ken that," said Willy, a hurt look spreading over his features. "So why go playing tricks on Willy?" The tears began to well up in the man's eyes, and his lower lip quivered.

Angus looked frantically at his sister.

"Jennie, please, can ye be explaining things to Willy? I cannae bear for him to think I'm deceiving him."

"I'm thinking, Angus," said his sister, looking with compassion at Willy, "that ye and Flinch would do well to scatter just now. Go call in at the castle while I work at calming the poor lad down and tending the needs of the dear old couple."

Angus could see the sense in this and said so.

"Let's trouble the poor soul no more with what he's not ever like to understand," concluded Jennie, opening the basket. "Willy, do ye like fresh-baked bread? It's still steaming from the oven."

Willy's face brightened. When his back was turned and Angus heard his, "Aye, Mistress Jennie. Ye ken I like to eat most everything," Angus ducked behind the edge of the cottage and still using his bow as a walking stick, he made his way to the west edge of town and to the castle.

5 FLINCH ANSWERS

Though Angus felt sorry for upsetting and confusing his friend Willy, he also was confident that Jennie would take care of the problem of the talking bird. She was good at things like that. And as always, he was eager for a visit with the earl.

The square battlements of Loudoun Castle came into view framed on either side by neat rows of beech trees lining the broad lane. Angus drew a deep breath of spring-scented air. He thought he detected a deep woody scent from the white blossoms of the earl's climbing rose that tumbled extravagantly over the gateway. Flinch dipped and bobbed at the starlings flying from tree to tree, and only with an effort did Angus keep the large bird perched on his shoulder.

Though he'd been told that a predecessor of the current laird designed the castle lane and gateway to look like Windsor Castle—in England—nevertheless, he felt somehow more secure, more hopeful about the future when the cause of the Covenant was supported by such a one as the Lord of Loudoun, fortified as he was by such an imposing fortress. He quickened his pace.

"Whence and whither bound?" barked a gruff voice as Angus drew near the imposing gate of the castle.

"From whence?—the moors," called Angus. "Whither? That one would seem rather obvious, I should think. I'm bound for the castle and a word with the laird. That is, if he'll see me."

"No more of yer cheek, Angus M'Kethe," said the young man at the gate. "And just who do ye be a-thinking ye are, strutting up to the laird's castle and demanding entrance? Speak, laddie."

"Och, William Cleland," retorted Angus, grinning as he leaned on his bow. "Do ye think ye're anything more than a lad yer very own self, then? Ye've only two years on me."

"Aye, but two years full of experience that ye've not had, nor never like to have if ye keep insisting on using that old bow of yers. It's not Frenchies we're fighting, here, laddie. These are Englishmen and traitor Scots with thick stubborn hide," said William, tapping the stock of his musket on the flagstones and giving his pouch of lead shot a rattle. "Aye, stubborn hide that demands a full charge of powder and plenty of hard-hammering lead ball."

"Ah, so," grinned Angus.

"Don't ye 'ah, so' me," said William. "Set aside that bow, and I'll train ye like a warrior Douglas. Have I told ye of my ancestors, the warrior Douglases?"

"Aye, ye hae done so many a time," replied Angus. "Aye, even in yer poetry, so ye have."

"Ah, so," said William, grinning. "Ye've brought along yer old bird, then."

"Aye."

"Whatever is he good for?" asked William, a question that Angus had more than once asked himself.

"Good for?" replied Angus. "While most crows are worse than a nuisance, Flinch here is so keen—"

"Keen?" snorted William. "Speak sense. It's a dumb bird, Angus."

"Aye, keen. So keen he is prepared to tell you in poetic alliteration"—Angus stroked Flinch's head, and looked imploringly into the bird's oily black eyes—"the two powers at odds with each other in Scotland."

The other boy slapped the thigh of his breeks and broke into laughter. William Cleland, sometime student at the University of St. Andrews, gifted poet, bold and passionate for the Covenant, was a young man much loved by his friends—and much hated by his enemies.

"Angus, ye talk like a daft limmer. I cannae think that the average Highlander in these parts could tell ye as much. But, go on. Prove to all that ye're as daft as yer crow. Go on, then."

Angus felt a trickle of perspiration descending the contours between his shoulder blades. He looked at Flinch's mysterious raven-colored eyes and clenched his teeth. This was after all a fairly new trick. Maybe it had been only a coincidence of sounds that had lined up in just the right order at just the right time. The likelihood of those sounds aligning just when Angus wanted them to—was remote in the extreme. He licked at a bead of sweat making its way down his cheek.

"Birds cannae speak, Angus," said William, grinning broadly. "And if I heard of a crow or any creature that could answer yer questions," he paused, his face contorting in mirth, "I'd call ye right about the bow—and hand over my musket."

Angus licked his lips.

"Flinch, what would ye say," he paused, grabbing the crow's beak and turning it toward him. "Och, Flinch. Pay attention, then. What would ye say are the two powers—*Flinch*, ye must look me in the eye—what then, would ye say are the two powers at odds with each other in Scotland?

"William Cleland, my bird cannae hear me with all yer

hooting and a-howling with laughter. If I could be asking ye for a bit of peace and quiet so as my bird can make out the question." Then turning again to Flinch, he said, "He doesnae think ye understand, Flinch." He suddenly had an idea. "Now then, what do ye *ken* are the two powers at odds with each other in Scotland. William, here, thinks ye're none too *keen* for such a question. But on such a question, I *ken* ye are *keen*."

"King and Kirk! King and Kirk!" replied Flinch, bowing stiffly.

It worked, thought Angus, grinning and offering his bird a kernel of corn.

William's mouth hung open in astonishment.

"Angus, ye're a bit off to be coming up with that." William shook his head and narrowed his eyes at the crow. "And I fear that some might be accusing ye of practicing the dark arts on the bird. They'll burn ye like the witches of Ayr. Ye must be careful, Angus."

"Och, William," said Angus. "No fear of that. He's as good a Presbyterian as any bird I hae ever kent."

William's face brightened. "I'd like to see the face of a superstitious Highlander after hearing yer bird speak. He'd think Flinch was a demon, and ye'd see his heels for certain." William slapped his friend on the back and laughed. "I donnae ken how ye've gone and done it, Angus, but I do ken ye'd not be dabbling away in the dark. But ye're stretching things to call that poetry."

"Aye, but I do call it an answer to my question, then," said Angus, extending his bow and pointing first at William's musket then back at himself.

William hugged his musket to his chest.

"Never. Ye've gone and tricked me, Angus."

"Och, William, I'll not be relieving ye of yer foul musket, ye ken that."

"Aye," said William, relieved.

"Flinch here is just imitating sounds, William. That's all.

And I learned about it from one of the laird's books. And, speaking of the laird, I'd best be going in to see him so I can get back and collect my sister."

"Jennie, is it?" said William, his eyes flashing with an interest that Angus had not detected before.

"Aye, Jennie," said Angus warily.

6 CHECKMATE?

"Yer move, lad," said James Campbell, Earl of Loudoun, as with a click and a tap he cleared away one of Angus's pawns.

Angus frowned as he studied the chessboard.

At first glance, the young peasant Scot wearing coarse homespun breeks and plaid, his bow and arrows on the floor beside him, a large crow perched on the carved head of a buck at the back of his chair, seemed out of place in the extreme. The well-appointed lord lounged in his great oak-paneled hall, under the staring eyes of dozens of antlered hunting trophies looking rigidly down on a fine collection of ancestral suits of armor and racks of weapons—muskets, pistols, pikes, and claymores—that hung at the ready about the hall. Nevertheless, the two chess players, so different in station and age, seemed to emit a companionable air of mutual enjoyment of each other's company, interrupted only occasionally by the "King and Kirk" of the even more incongruous member of the scene—the crow.

The earl sprang from a long line of Christian Campbells of Loudoun. More than 150 years ago, James IV, King of Scotland, had summoned the present earl's ancestor John Campbell to answer charges of heresy for his efforts in the early reformation of the Church. And he was accused—an accusation he wore as a badge of honor—of being a member of the Lollards of Kyle, the poor preachers and followers of John Wycliffe.

"A bit of Dutch chocolate, perhaps," offered the earl with the hint of a triumphal smile.

He thinks he's got me this time, thought Angus as he bit into the thick, brown sweetness and felt the enchanting trickle of the chocolate down his throat.

"And how goes yer reading, lad?" continued the earl, sitting back and crossing his legs.

Angus lifted his eyes from the chessboard. "I like the book very much, indeed, yer lairdship."

"It is a most innovative allegory, is it not?"

"An allegory, sir?"

"Aye, allegory," said the earl, leaning forward as if eager to explain. "Have I not instructed ye in the conventions of allegory?"

"No, but might I read it again before we do?"

"Aye, lad. Read it again and again. But, remember, it reads more like metaphor—like pictures and images of higher things."

Again Angus studied the chessboard. He did want to discuss the book with the earl, just not right this moment. The first five times he had played the earl, the earl had won. But in the last three years, when the game was up, the earl's king almost always lay prostrate on the board.

"Ye ken these Highlanders plaguing the valley?" said the earl in a conversational tone.

"I ken they're plaguing the valley," replied Angus.

"Aye, but did ye ken many of them play chess? Did ye ken that, Angus?

Angus looked up in genuine surprise.

"I didnae ken this," he replied.

"They claim to hae started the game," continued the earl.

"But I think they might be a wee bit mistaken about that." He paused, looking intently at Angus. "I'm told that they've a clan chief among them who, like ye, is only rarely beaten. What think ye of that, Angus, lad?"

"Ah, so," replied Angus, looking absently at the earl. He shook his head firmly. *I must concentrate*, he told himself, narrowing his eyes at the checkered board set into the richly carved table—Dutch made, like the chocolate.

The earl steepled his fingers, and his eyes darted from the board to his young opponent's face. He liked Angus—and he liked to win at chess, but just now these likes seemed increasingly more at odds with each other.

Angus stole a quick glance at the earl, then again he studied the board. If he moved his knight forward and to the right flank of the earl's king—that would never do; he'd be gobbled up by the earl's bishop. And Angus knew that if he moved his castle, in but two moves the earl would put him in check.

He won't expect a direct attack from my king, thought Angus, his mind rapidly running over the narrowing strategic options left to the earl if Angus made such a bold move.

"Ye put me in mind of my late father," the earl's voice broke in on Angus's calculations.

"Aye," said Angus absently.

"Aye, it were in 1641, he admonished the erstwhile king Charles I."

Angus wondered if the earl was trying to distract him.

The earl cleared his voice and looked up at the high carved vaulting of the ceiling. "Said he to the king, 'As those who are sworn to defend our religion, our recourse must be only in the God of Jacob, for our refuge.'" The earl's voice rose in a lilting passion. "'Who is King of kings and Lord of lords,

and by whom kings do reign and princes decree justice.' So he said, and before a king."

"King and Kirk!" screeched Flinch.

"Aye, yer bird has the best of vocabulary, Angus," laughed the earl. He held a morsel of chocolate toward Flinch, who flew across to the arm of the earl's chair and gulped it eagerly down.

"Still yer move, I believe," said the earl, nodding at the board.

"Aye," said Angus, trying to bring his mind back to the game. With a plunk of the carved figure on the hardwood board, he advanced his king.

The earl sat up, ran his hand through his graying hair, and scowled at the diminishing figures on the board. Swaying and bobbing, Flinch kept an eye on the plate of chocolate.

"Are ye sure?" he said, eyeing Angus narrowly.

"Aye. As sure as one can be in war."

The earl advanced a pawn with a click. Then he sat back against a tapestry cushion and said, "My father was a bold man before the king, he was."

"Aye," agreed Angus, his eyes now glued to the board. Two moves and he would have the earl in checkmate.

"My father went on in his speaking to the king and said to the effect, 'Betwixt Kirk and State there is a contradistinction in power and in officers. And though formally different and distinct, yet is there so strict and necessary a conjunction betwixt religion and justice, as the one cannot flourish without the other.' " The earl again sat up and brought his fist down on the table with a bang. Angus clutched at the rattling figures. " 'Therefore,' continued my father before the king, 'Kirk and State must stand and fall, live and die together.' What think ye of that, Angus?"

Angus worked at shifting the chessmen back to the center of their squares.

"Now, then, Angus," said the earl, squinting critically at the board. "Was not my king in that square, there?"

"I think not, yer lairdship," said Angus, eyeing the earl.

Flinch swayed side to side as if in a kind of trance; the object of his meditation appeared to be the chocolate.

"Aye, perhaps ye're right, lad." The earl passed his hand across the deepening furrows on his brow.

"Yer father was right, I'm thinking," said Angus, his eyes making a final survey of the board. He broke off a hunk of chocolate and sat back.

The earl blinked nervously at the board.

"We'd hae none of our present woes in the Kirk," said Angus, helping himself to another piece of the earl's chocolate, "if justice reigned in the state."

"Aye," agreed the earl. "And the greatest human cause of woe in the Kirk," he paused, drumming his fingers on the table, his brow furrowed at the chessboard, "is that Covenant-breaking archbishop."

"Sharp?" replied Angus. "Not bloody Claverhouse?"

"Claverhouse is a monster and make no mistake. But it's Sharp who stirs up the cesspool of Claverhouse's evil. Aye, Sharp's the man, and sharp he makes our woes."

"For how long?" asked Angus.

"There's a question, indeed," replied the earl. "But God in heaven alone kens the answer, Angus. Meanwhile, we wait patiently on God's mercy and pray that the time will be shortened." More finger drumming on the table. "Some say that Sharp's own time may be shortened. And I fear there are those among us who claim to follow the Covenant who just might lift a hand to help shorten his time."

"Ye mean murder him?"

"Aye, I fear it."

"But then the king goes and props yet another brute in Sharp's place," said Angus. "And the new archbishop could be worse still."

"Worse than Sharp? Believing that takes more imagination than I have—though, mind ye, I'd never support murdering him."

Angus frowned, the chess game nearly forgotten.

"But would ye support armed resistance of Claverhouse and his murdering dragoons," he asked, "which means the killing of men on their side? Would ye then?"

"Aye," replied the earl, looking sharply at Angus. "But taking up a sword in defense of women and bairns, and all gathered peacefully to worship the Lord, there's no murder in that, lad."

"If our hearts be right, there's no murder in that," Angus replied softly, as if to himself. He gazed unseeingly at the chessboard.

"So where, then," he continued, looking earnestly at the earl and leaning forward, his elbows now on the table, "lies the line between murder and killing in a just cause?"

The earl looked up from his brooding at the chessboard.

"If the king, the English, the wild Highlanders, the Covenant-breaking Scots led by Sharp and his hosts—" He brought his long index finger down on the table with each word. "I say, if they send the likes of the brute Claverhouse to descend in arms on peacefully gathered folk, then we who are strong and can wield the weapons of war"—here he flung his arm in a sweeping gesture about the hall—"must, I say, *must* rise and fight. To do otherwise is base and cowardly—though our cause would more likely prevail with the aid of men like Richard Cameron and the faithful exiles in Holland. Nevertheless, lad, to defend the weak with our strength—is to obey God. There's yer line."

"And may I never cross it," said Angus simply.

"Aye, may none of us," agreed the earl.

"What happened to yer father after speaking so boldly to the king?" asked Angus.

"Och, there's many a time when I wonder about kings—and bishops," said the earl, looking forlornly over the chessboard. "Charles I and his Archbishop Laud mocked my father and, in violation of his safe conduct, threw him in the Tower of London. Then, without legal trial, the king ordered my father's head to be struck off by nine of the clock next morning."

The chess game all but forgotten, Angus stared at the earl's sober eyes. "I didnae ken this story, yer lairdship. And I am most awfully sorry for it."

"The king wanted his cruelty kept quiet," continued the earl. "But the Lord thwarted the schemes of Charles, thanks to a good man who risked his life for my father's. Knowing the injustice of the king's order, the lieutenant of the Tower, William Balfour, went himself to the king with the Christian Marquess of Hamilton to plead on behalf of my father. After considerable fuming and ranting, the king tore up the execution order. A month later my father was freed."

"I'm glad of it," said Angus.

"My father commanded a brigade of horse and played no small part in efforts to bring Charles to terms in the first wave of the Civil War. After which, my father so effectively urged unity and peace between king and Covenanting Scotland and her Parliament that Charles made my father Chancellor of all Scotland."

"From scheming to lift off his head," said Angus, wonderingly, "to making him head of Scotland. My father would say, 'The king's heart is in the hand of the Lord, and he turns it withersoever he wills.'"

"And yer father would be right in saying it."

"I'm wondering: if we had more men like yer father in Scotland," said Angus, "we might hae reached some peaceful settlement with the king long before now."

"Och, Angus, ye ken not the ways of Stuart kings," said

the earl. "Charles fought on against his Puritan Parliament and finally dissolved Parliament all together. Meanwhile, my father accompanied worthy Rutherford and the Scots Commissioners to the Westminster Assembly. Battles raged on, and when things looked hopeless for Charles and the Royalists, he surrendered to the Scots army at Newcastle. My father spoke again to the hard-hearted king warning him that upon his refusal to submit to Parliament 'all will rise against ye as one man and will depose ye, and set up another government. They will charge us to deliver up yer Majesty to them, and upon yer refusal, we shall be obliged to settle religion and peace without ye.' "

"And still he refused?"

"Aye, with hauteur and high disdain. Finally, Parliament and Cromwell beheaded Charles I, King of England and Scotland—though I cannae go along with regicide, he was a king who deserved what he got. Ye ken the rest: betrayed by the English, we Scots crowned Charles's son; whereupon, Cromwell invaded Scotland, and, in 1660, Charles II was restored to the throne—"

"—And hasnae stopped wreaking vengeance on Covenanters ever since," said Angus. "But what happened to yer father?"

"Died in a most Christian manner in Edinburgh in 1652," said the earl. "And his remains await the resurrection here at the castle with his ancestors."

"He missed out on all our present woes from Charles II, then," said Angus.

"Aye," agreed the earl, now tapping the crown of his beleaguered king with his index finger. "But ye, Angus—ye've hemmed me in and given me woes a-plenty yerself, just now."

"Ah, so?" said Angus innocently.

"If I move my bishop and take yer pawn, there," said the

earl, with the rolling-eyed look of a cornered buck, "ye sweep in on my knight with yer castle like the plague and then—I'm in check."

"If ye'll be forgiving me for saying so," said Angus. "I believe, sir, ye'd be in checkmate."

"Nae, nae, not checkmate, is it?" said the earl.

Suddenly, Flinch broke free from his trancelike state, and with a flurry of feathers and a greedy cawing, the bird dove at the plate of chocolate. Chessmen flew in all directions and clattered onto the flagstone floor. Angus was never quite sure if it had been his bird's wings and tail or the earl's frantic efforts to save the chocolate that cleared the chessboard; either way, the game was over. Flinch retreated behind the steel shanks of a standing suit of armor, a slab of chocolate pinned menacingly to the floor under his claws. Chocolate dribbled from his beak as he gorged away on the scavenged sweetness.

"Pity, lad," laughed the earl as on their knees he and Angus gathered up the scattered chess pieces. "And I think ye just might hae beaten me—the very one that taught ye all ye ken of chess. But then we'll never ken for certain sure, now will we?"

"Aye, yer lairdship," agreed Angus. "But we live to war again."

"Aye, so we do," agreed the earl, his face growing sober. "So we do."

7 DESTROY THEM?

The last pale shafts of light lingered in the narrow window on the northwest corner of the M'Kethe croft. Angus sat under the window on a stone niche built for just this purpose, his knees raised, feet on the edge of the niche, his elbows propped on his knees, and in his raised hands the last of the amber light fell warmly on the pages of the earl's book.

The rhythmic clicking of knitting needles, the hiss of burning peat, the low voices, his mother humming a psalm tune, and an occasional burst of youthful laughter faded into a gently mingled backdrop of sound, so conducive for reading. Angus had finished the book some days ago and had decided to reread it before discussing it with his father and the earl—and, if he could find one of them, the fugitive ministers, Mr. King or Mr. Douglas. The pleasant background noises receded further as he read:

> . . . At last, when every man started back for fear of the armed men, Christian saw a man of a very stout countenance come up . . . he saw the man draw his sword,

> and put a helmet on his head, and rush toward the door upon the armed men, who laid upon him with deadly force.

"Uncle Angus's eyes are muckle big ones," came a child's voice, vaguely intruding on the conflict, so vivid at that moment in Angus's imagination.

He leaned closer to the fading light of the window and squinted at the page.

> But the man fell to cutting and hacking most fiercely. So, after he had received and given many wounds to those that attempted to keep him out, he cut his way through them all and pressed forward into the palace.

"What is it ye're so all wide-eyed and gaping at, Angus?" called his mother, never missing a beat with her knitting needles.

He raised his head slowly, closed the book and joined the family, each in their place around the hearth. Most evenings when the day's work was behind them, the growing M'Kethe family gathered around the warm glow of the hearth in the croft of the patriarch of the clan. Thirteen years had brought many changes in the family, not all of them unexpected, and as these changes contributed to the growth of the family, they were received with joy and gratitude.

Fiona, Angus's older sister, had married Duncan's good friend, Jamie, who long ago had taken "Crookshank" for his preferred name. He wore the name as a badge of honor. Four years ago Fiona was delivered of twins. At the urging of their families, the couple had named their twin son and daughter, Sandy and Mary, after their grandparents. Then, to their great joy, another girl had been born to them in January two years past. However, within days of birth, she developed a feeble rasping cough, and to their great sorrow, after a month of infant tears, she died in her mother's arms, her coughing now ended and her little tears dry. Her parents' were not. With aching hearts, they laid her frail little body to rest in the moor sod behind their croft.

"What is it ye're reading, Uncle?" the eight-year-old voice of Angus's nephew, Malcolm, broke in on his thoughts.

" 'Tis a tale of the King's Highway," replied Angus, showing Malcolm the book.

"It must be about a road that leads to woe and trouble, then," said the boy, knowingly.

"Nae, Malcolm. 'Tis a book about the best of Kings."

"And are there battles in it, then?" asked the boy, eagerly drawing himself up next to his uncle.

"Aye, there are, indeed."

"Maybe ye'd be reading it to me, then," said the boy.

"I'm sure he gets enough of battles and weapons from his father," came a young woman's voice, accompanied by the woody clicking of knitting needles, out of the shadows.

"And if he's to grow up to defend the Crown rights of the Redeemer," interjected Duncan, adding peat to the hissing fire, "he'll be needing more stories of that ilk, m'love, that's certain."

"Aye, if he's taught to love his enemies all the while." Angus's father's voice rose and fell with that mysterious mixture of strength and gentleness that Angus knew sprang from the depths of his father's character. He studied the broad shoulders, the work-hardened hands now stroking the auburn locks of his granddaughter's hair. Angus felt such a mixture of emotions with his father: sometimes wonder, sometimes even fear, but all mingled with a certain pulsing aspiration.

"Aye," said Duncan, "and to do good to those who despitefully use him."

"Aye, indeed," said Angus's mother, her clicking suspended for an instant. "And we with despiteful users on every side—there's no fear of our running short of them."

"But however do we reconcile obedience to the king," came the young woman's earnest voice from the shadows again, "with defending truth and justice for the oppressed?"

Angus looked at the young woman in the shadows, his sister-in-law. He remembered snatches of her story, seldom retold now. She had once lived in the king's city of Edinburgh; she'd been a faithful adherent to prelacy—to bishops, prayer books, and to the king as head of the Church. Her father had been head jailer to the King's Counsel—a bloody brood of unjust judges, tormentors of Lowland Scots who adhered to the National Covenant, and who swore their loyalty to King Jesus only as head of the Church. Hers was a bitter, ironic tale. Early in the year 1667, her father was accused of complicity in a certain rescue of a Covenanter prisoner awaiting execution for his part in the Pentland Rising. Her father was arrested, thrown in the Tollbooth, a prisoner in his own prison—but there was to be little fear of rats and protracted, festering prison diseases for him. After a hasty trial, in which, with oaths and curses, he swore his innocence, they dragged him out to the public Grassmarket where he was hanged. His daughter, Lindsay, numb with horror, knowing her own part in that escape, looked on. Her mother was whisked away by Highland relations, and it fell to a certain fisherman to get Lindsay out of the city before more questions could be asked. That fisherman knew no better place for her than with his brother's family now hiding some miles away in the windswept moors near Loudoun Hill.

Twelve winters had past since Lindsay came to live with them, but it had taken no more than four of those years to see that Duncan and Lindsay had formed a certain attachment—these kinds of things made Angus a bit squirmy. That attachment and marriage, however, was not a daisy-chain, swooning one. Frequent discussions of a passionate nature ensued between the young couple: discussions about bishops, kneeling in church, and about Christmas. But under the umpirial guidance of Angus's mother and father, the couple had grown to love each other deeply and devotedly. Their only child Malcolm had just marked his eighth year, and was a particular friend of his Uncle Angus.

"Aye, Lindsay," said Angus's father. "How to honor the king—and honor the King of kings all at the same go. Figure that out and ye have what Holy Scripture calls sanctification—holiness, without which no man shall see the King in all his glory and splendor on the Great Day. But, God be praised, we aren't left to figure it out on our own. We have the Word of God and we have the Spirit of God showing us the way of holiness. But donnae let's go expecting that the way to glory will be trod without suffering, without our being beset on every side by God's enemies."

From where Angus's father sat at the trestle table, candlelight now flickered and cast his broad shadow behind him against the stones of the wall. A hush had come over the room, and only Angus's mother continued her knitting, slower now than before. Sandy M'Kethe reached for his big Bible as he continued.

"If our Lord and Redeemer, the author of our salvation, was made perfect through suffering, who are we to go around all surprised at our sufferings. Ours are ordained by a loving heavenly Father that we might learn perseverance, that we might learn to lay our troubles at the all-capable feet of one who promises to bear them all for us."

"But, Father," said Jennie, setting her wool down and moving to his side at the table. "It's so much easier to talk of suffering"—her voice trailed away for a moment—"than to actually face it with courage when . . . when it's no longer time for the talking of it but for the enduring of it."

"Aye, lass. So it is with all things. Theory is always easier than practice. Talking of shearing is always easier than the shearing itself, and so it is with talking of knitting a lovely pair of fine wool socks for the winter, and the actual doing of the knitting. Ye ken all this, my dear ones. But ye must ken that without the theory, the practice'll never come right in the day of trial."

"But, Father," said Angus. "Is there no place, then, for fighting, for resisting the ones who come to harm us, to take away our sheep, our homes?"

"Aye, and our Covenanted freedom to worship God?" added Mary M'Kethe.

"Not to mention," said Duncan, rising to his feet, "our lives. Many have died before us in this struggle."

"Aye, as will many more, if God does not come to our aid soon," said Mary M'Kethe, her needles now silent.

"God will arise and put all our enemies to flight," said Sandy M'Kethe, in that way he had of almost singing the Psalter in his replies. "But he's under no obligation to do that when we want him to. Thus, 'not my will but thine be done,' we pray. Meanwhile, we obey him and pray for strength to do our duty today. Have no fear. He'll give us strength for tomorrow's trials. So, let's us leave it with him, then."

With his big work-hardened hands, Sandy M'Kethe opened the Bible in that ceremonious way of his, with wonder and a slight quickening of the breath as if handling a fragrant rose or taking up in his great arms a newborn infant.

"Let us worship God," he said. After leading them in a prayer that would make the hardest heart weep, they sang a psalm together. "Now hear the Word of the Lord," he said, "as we continue reading in the history of redemption, Second Samuel twenty-two."

Angus, with Malcolm curled up on his lap, closed his eyes and let the words wash over his mind and heart as his father's voice, rising in lilting passion, read King David's ancient song of praise.

" 'The Lord is my rock, my fortress . . . from violent men you save me . . . The Lord thundered from heaven; the voice of the Most High resounded. He shot his arrows and scattered the enemies, bolts of lightning and routed them.' "

Angus's eyes shot open at this point. He suddenly felt his mind revolving around those words. They mingled with the book he'd been reading and began to form themselves into poetry of his own. He would write it down later.

Our God shall rise with power and might
And put his foe, the Fiend, to flight.
Like lightning bolts, he shoots his shafts;
Then in the pit his foes he casts.

His father's voice continued:

" 'It is God who arms me with strength . . .
He trains my hand for battle;
My arm can bend a bow of bronze.' "

Angus knew how difficult it was to handle a full-sized yew bow. How could anyone bend a bow made of bronze? What kind of strength, he wondered, would be needed to do that? But what his father read next made him almost dump Malcolm off his lap.

" 'I pursued my enemies and crushed them;
I did not turn back until they were all destroyed.
I crushed them completely . . .

You made my enemies turn their backs in flight
And I destroyed my foes . . .
I beat them as fine as the dust of the earth;
I pounded and trampled them like mud in the streets . . .
The Lord lives! . . .
Exalted be God . . . my Savior! . . .
Who set me free from my enemies . . .' "

His father's voice had risen to a fever pitch of praise, and now the room was silent, save for the sputtering of sheep-tallow candles and the hissing of the peat fire.

Duncan broke the silence first.

"Aye, and just when I think I've got it all figured out," he said, gazing into the fire and shaking his head. After the jolt Angus had given him, Malcolm slid off Angus's lap and crawled up on his father's lap near the fire. "Ye go and read something like that from the Holy Book."

"How does crushing foes completely," asked Angus, "work with loving enemies?"

"And that bit about trampling them," said Jennie, a bewildered furrow to her brow, "like mud in the streets. What is the theory here, Father, and how is it we go about putting it into practice?"

"Is it high rising metaphor?" asked Angus, leaning over his father's broad shoulders and running his eyes down the text again. "Or is it something less, or something—more?"

"Rhyme," said Jennie, absently, giving the agreed upon signal designed to rein in Angus's tendency, from time to time, to speak in rhyme.

"Sorry," mumbled Angus with a grimace.

Their father took a deep breath and held it for a moment before expelling it and forming his reply.

"Every word in this book is from God above and for our

profit. True as that is and remains, I donnae claim to understand all the ways of the Lord herein described."

"Aye, Father," said Angus. "But it would seem that beleaguered on every side as we are by the enemies of the Kirk, we must understand what this means. We hae to ken if God is speaking in figures and symbols here, or if he actually wants us doing it."

"I can think of some of those that claim to own the Covenant," said their mother, "who would particularly like this bit of Scripture."

"Aye," agreed Jennie. "Some there are that just want an excuse for killing of the king's men, English or Scots."

"Aye, the likes of John Burly Balfour of Kinloch spring readily to mind," said their mother, jabbing her knitting needles into a ball of wool yarn. "His kind make trouble for us all, they do."

"Mary, m'love," said Sandy M'Kethe in a gently reproving tone.

"But their hatred and love of killing," said Angus, "isn't the same as what King David is singing about in this text. He's not calling us to kill for its own sake, then."

"Aye, lad. And we're sure to get it wrong," said their father, "if we decide what's true by running from radicals on one side or the other."

"But what do we do, Father?" asked Jennie.

"Aye, the Bible is a doing book," added Duncan.

Their father steepled his hands and rested his chin on his fingers. No one spoke as he silently reread the passage. Angus knew that his father would be reading and crying out to the Lord for wisdom all at the same time. He didn't imagine there were many waking hours in his father's life now that were not filled with just such crying out.

At last he spoke.

"I'm inclined to think that if we lived peaceful, comfortable lives, free of tyranny, pillage, and death from an unjust government . . ." he paused, firelight flickering in his eyes as he seemed to be gazing into the glimmers of other times and other places. "I say, that if we looked at this text from that vantage point alone, we would find it all metaphor, all symbol."

"Do ye mean, then, Father," began Angus, "that the battle is a only a picture of battle with our sins, and that would make the enemies the world, the flesh, and the devil?"

"Aye, something along those lines, then," agreed his father.

"But, Father, I cannae even imagine living in a place with such peace and comforts," said Angus. "Do ye ken of such a place?"

"Aye, it's called heaven," said Mary M'Kethe, nodding knowingly.

"Och, and our Scotland under Charles II," said Duncan, "is much more akin to hell than heaven."

"Father, do ye think that David—it was David who penned the poetry, after all," said Angus. "Do ye think *he* thought it was all metaphor?"

"Aye, an important question, indeed, Angus, my lad," said Sandy M'Kethe.

"I cannae imagine," said Jennie, shaking her head, flashes of russet brown highlights shimmering in her hair, "that David, the giant killer, the warrior, the one about whom the young women sang that he'd slain his tens of thousands, I cannae imagine *he* thought this just metaphor."

"Nor can I," agreed their father. "Nor can I."

8 THE DUEL

(May 2, 1679)

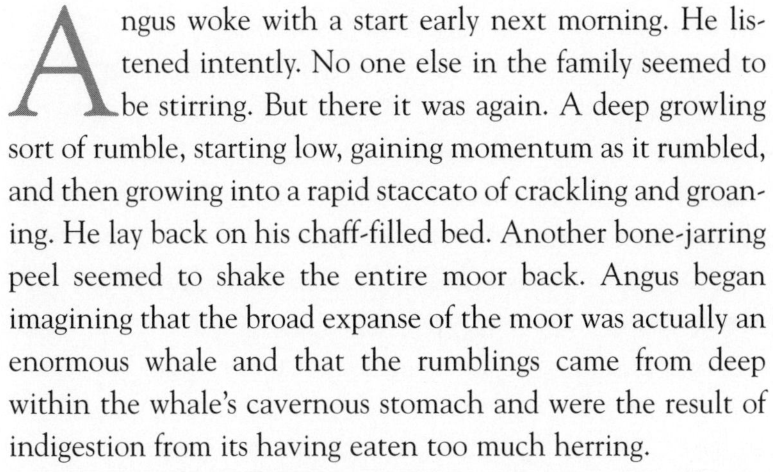

Angus woke with a start early next morning. He listened intently. No one else in the family seemed to be stirring. But there it was again. A deep growling sort of rumble, starting low, gaining momentum as it rumbled, and then growing into a rapid staccato of crackling and groaning. He lay back on his chaff-filled bed. Another bone-jarring peel seemed to shake the entire moor back. Angus began imagining that the broad expanse of the moor was actually an enormous whale and that the rumblings came from deep within the whale's cavernous stomach and were the result of indigestion from its having eaten too much herring.

A white flash of light pulsed for an instant through the narrow windows of the croft and penetrated the predawn dimness with elongated shafts of floodlight that quickly disappeared.

Then it came to him: the duel. His father had not wanted Angus and Duncan to have their duel because the noise of the musket fire would arouse the suspicion of the Highlanders in the valley, or of Claverhouse and his prowling dragoons, some of whom might come and investigate. But no one could hear a musket in a thunderstorm! Angus flew out of bed. Hopping on one leg, he pulled on his breeks, wrapped his plaid over his shoulder, grabbed up his bow and arrows, and tiptoed out of the croft.

He made his way in the darkness over to the narrow window of his brother's croft. For a moment he hesitated, the rising wind wiping his hair across his face and sending his plaid in a swirling spiral behind him. To block the wind, they could shoot in the hollow just up the moor and to the southeast, but they'd have to hurry. The rain would fall in torrents from the sounds of it, and there'd be no chance that Duncan's musket would fire in heavy rain.

Angus drew his dirk from his waist belt, and lightly with the tip of the blade, he tapped at the window. "Tap, tap, tap." He waited. Duncan would not be thrilled about being awakened by his younger brother. "Tap, tap, tap." But Angus really wanted to test his skill against a musket, and Duncan was a crack shot with the musket. "Tap, tap, tap." This time Angus used the hilt of his dirk.

A squinting, freckled face surrounded by a mop of red hair, frenzied from sleep, appeared only inches away on the other side of the narrow windowpane. Angus put on his best smile and waved. Duncan's eyes narrowed into dark slits, and his mouth pursed into a thin, hard line.

"The du-el," Angus mouthed, holding up an imaginary musket and convulsing with the imaginary retort. "Th-u-n-d-er. Sh-oo-t-ing. No s-oun-d." He put his fingers in his ears and nodded encouragingly.

Duncan rolled his eyes and shook his head in disgust at his younger brother. He signaled with his head toward the door of the croft and disappeared from view.

"Angus M'Kethe, ye're daft as yer crow," hissed Duncan moments later at the doorway. But he pulled on his coarse jacket and reached for his musket as he said it.

"I'll go get Father," said Angus, spinning on his heel. He was desperately afraid that the thunder might end before they could shoot—he frowned up at the angry clouds—or that rain might make it impossible for Duncan to shoot at all. "We've got to hurry," he called over his shoulder.

***

"Duncan, gather up yer claymore," called Sandy M'Kethe as the dueling party gathered in the dim half-light of early morning. He carried his claymore at his belt, and a small bale of wool on his shoulder.

"Ye actually think yer bow can stand up against Duncan's musket?" asked Jennie as they made their way farther up the moor. She insisted on coming along, and Malcolm, awakened by Angus's tapping, had begged to come, too. He held his father's hand and stifled a gaping, toothy yawn as he scurried to keep up.

"Wait for me!" called Lindsay from the doorway of the croft. "I'll not be missing out on the excitement."

"Ye're welcome to see all," said Duncan, smiling as the party waited while Lindsay joined them.

"Can Angus's bow stand with the musket?" Jennie asked again.

"There's but one way to find out," said their father.

"Aye, but I just hope the rain holds off for a wee bit," said Angus after another peel of thunder rumbled across the moor.

"Grandfather," said Malcolm, panting under the weight of his father's claymore. "Why claymores—for a duel with musket and bow?"

"Whatever the outcome of the duel, my lad, yer Uncle Angus needs practice with the claymore."

Angus groaned inwardly. There had been a time long ago

when he had felt a certain fascination for the claymore—as a child he'd even tried to filch Duncan's claymore in the night. Those days were gone. No, he didn't relish the idea of close fighting with swords; fact is, he thought fighting with swords a bit uncivilized and merely a last resort, an indicator that all other means—by which he meant bows and arrows—had somehow failed. For Angus, however, these thoughts of fighting and battle remained firmly in the realm of theory; shooting crows in flight was hardly on a par with real combat.

Another drum roll of thunder echoed through the shadowy valley below.

"Does this suit ye, lads?" asked their father when they reached the southeast hollow.

Angus looked anxiously at the darkening clouds churning overhead. *If the rain would only hold off*, he thought, ratcheting his longbow against his leg and setting the bowstring tightly in place. With a *twang*, he tested the tautness.

"Who has the first go?" asked Duncan.

"Ye may go first," said Angus, casting another nervous glance at the ominous clouds.

"No," said Duncan. "Ye cooked up this scheme, brother. Ye go."

Their father stretched a scrap of cloth over the bale, and with a piece of charcoal, he drew a circle the size of a man's head and two other successively smaller ones, each inside the other, the smallest no larger than the eye of a full-grown beltie bull. He strode off, his lips silently counting off fifty paces. Then, he set the target against a rise and strode back.

"Proceed, Angus," he said with a clipped nod of his head. "Three shots each."

Angus selected an arrow, narrowed his eyes at the target, wet the goose feathers deliberately with his tongue, and looked for a moment at Duncan's sober face—his eyes darted from Angus to the target and back again. *He's worried*, Angus thought, a smug little tug pulling at the corners of his mouth. *As well he ought to be*. With that, he set the arrow on the string and, in one steady motion, drew, leveled the shaft and—

A deafening crash of thunder broke across the moor and ricocheted through the hollow as the arrow flew from Angus's bow. It mushed harmlessly into the peaty sod, fully a handbreadth from the bale of wool.

Angus blinked in confusion. He could hit crows in flight, but here he was, when it really mattered, he couldn't even hit a bale of wool. He felt an almost overwhelming urge to explain: it was the thunder, the dim light, the despoiling hopes of his brother upsetting his ability to concentrate. It had to be one of these excuses.

"Too bad," said Duncan. " 'Twas the thunder that drew ye off, lad. When ye shoot a musket, ye grow accustomed to the sound of thunder."

Bewildered, Angus stepped to Jennie's side while Duncan began the process of loading his musket. With a bitter scowl, Angus critically inspected his bowstring. It had to be some flaw in the string—or maybe it was a bad fletching job on the arrow. How could his bow have failed him now?

Then, almost involuntarily, Angus found his mind revolving around verse: something he'd read in the Psalter, maybe in the earl's book, but from wherever, he began composing, counting meter on his fingers. Maybe it was all finally just a means of escape—or worse yet, an expression of sour grapes. He shook his head at that thought and looked up the moor.

I do not trust, then, in my bow,

—seemed a fitting first line under the circumstances. He looked again at his bow.

I do not trust, then, in my bow,
For God will hurl in hell his foe.

He eyed his brother. He wasn't exactly thinking of Duncan as his foe—not really. And then from deep within a mind and soul filled daily with Holy Scripture—read, explained, applied, and practiced by those closest to him—Angus found these words forming in his mind and sobering him.

Ye foes, to Christ give glory now:
For now or then to God ye'll bow.

Casual whistling suddenly interrupted his musings. He looked at his brother.

As he loaded his musket, Duncan whistled with studied nonchalance. Angus tried to look unconcerned by clasping his hands and leaning on his bow, but he felt the heat rising on his face as he watched the ordeal.

First, Duncan poured powder from his premeasured bandolier down the muzzle. Then, for what seemed like several minutes, he packed it all down the muzzle with wadding, using quick sliding strokes with his ramrod. He selected a lead ball from his pouch, looked at it for a moment, and thrust it back into the pouch—lead ball was too expensive to use for practice shooting. Searching around on the ground, he selected a stone the size of the end of his middle finger and dropped it down the barrel. Then began the more delicate task of priming the musket. Duncan's face glowed orange as he bent over the lock assembly and blew on the match cord. He eyed Angus as he waited for the red glow that would tell him he was ready to plunge the match into the firing pan and actually, then—if all went well—fire the musket.

This proves it, Angus thought, his cheeks glowing red from frustration and embarrassment. Angus guessed that even if he were aiming with care, he could have gotten off six or seven arrows in the length of time it was taking his brother to fire one shot—and a pebble shot at that. Jennie squeezed his arm reassuringly and gave her brother a gently reproving look that said she understood exactly what he was thinking.

Lifting the heavy musket to his shoulder, Duncan, at last, leveled it toward the bale and pulled the trigger. With a sort of click and delay, and almost as an afterthought, a coughing roar sounded from the muzzle, and a cloud of blue-gray engulfed the shooter and then blew in the onlookers' faces. For several minutes, no one could see anything through the smoke.

"Och!" cried Jennie, coughing and fanning the acrid smoke from her face.

"Boom, boom!" cried Malcolm, jumping up and down and clapping his hands together with glee. "Ye got 'em all, Father!"

"And any lads ye missed," said Lindsay, "will be deaf for life."

Angus's eyes smarted as he squinted through the haze, trying to make out what damage his brother did or did not do to the target. He thought he felt a drop of rain on his hot cheek.

They walked toward the target through the spreading smoke that now drifted in foul-smelling banks throughout the hollow, Angus, at one and the same time, eager and reluctant to see the results. Malcolm, coughing and sneezing, ran ahead.

"Ye got it! Ye got it!" his voice came through the blue haze.

Angus tried to control the ugly fumes rising in his heart and creeping into every corner of his features. He didn't like the way he was feeling, but he seemed unable to do anything about it, at least not at the moment.

"Outer ring shot," announced Angus's father without emotion. "Yer shot, Angus."

Eager to remove any reminder of his bad shooting, Angus grabbed his arrow and pulled. The moist sod seemed to tug at the other end of the arrow, as if mocking him. Another raindrop struck his face, this time square on the nose. He brushed it impatiently aside.

Back at the shooting line, Angus waited until the thunder rumbled into a moment of disgruntled silence. He had to hit the mark. He had to.

"Put all else aside," whispered Jennie in his ear, "and think of only one thing—shooting. That'd be my advice to ye, brother."

He peered through the haze, left eye screwed shut and right eye blinking back the smoke. Angus set his arrow on the string; he felt the bowstring bite into the fingers of his right hand—he had to be steady—his left elbow locked and rigid, the muscles of his right arm tense and hard.

Twang! Silently, his shaft left behind it a thin corridor of swirling air, made visible through the blue smoke. *Thwonk!* The arrow shimmied as it struck true in the bale.

But *where* did it strike the target? Angus blinked eagerly, trying to see through the haze. More raindrops hit his face, too many now to wipe away.

"Bravo! Uncle!" called Malcolm, though he seemed somewhat less enthusiastic, and Angus vaguely wondered if it was all finally about the big noise, the smoke, and smells.

Angus strode rapidly toward the target, his eyes sorting hungrily through the haze. Then he could see it all. He exhaled an enormous lungful of air and smiled. Bull's-eye. Admittedly, not the prettiest bull's-eye, off on the extreme left side of the center ring, but nevertheless, a bull's-eye. The others caught up and inspected the target.

"A wonderful shot, Angus," said Jennie, looping her arm in his. Raindrops moistened her face and stood out like delicate beads in her hair as she grinned encouragingly at her brother.

"Aye, Uncle, ye got 'em for certain sure!" exclaimed Malcolm.

"There is something to be saying, Angus," said Lindsay, a playful smirk on her lips, "for the peace and quiet of the bow. After all, maybe killing that's peaceful and quiet like is better killing."

Duncan looked sideways at his wife, then at Angus. "Not bad," he said shortly. "No, brother, not bad—for a second shot, that is. But ye'd best remove yer arrow before I take my next shot, though I think I can still see my way clear for the center of the target."

"Aye, 'tis shading left of center," agreed their father, grinning through his beard, now thick with droplets of rain that trickled into a saturated fringe.

By the time the party had returned to the shooting line, and after Duncan began the process of preparing his musket for loading, priming, and firing, rain fell in torrents. With a hiss Duncan's match cord fizzled, and with a feeble wafting of smoke, the orange glow died out and only a charred cord remained.

"Hmm. And then there's the quiet," said Lindsay, stroking her wet locks pensively, "without the killing."

"Aye, then. That about settles that," said Duncan. "Maybe some other day I'll get my second shot, as ye've had yers, Angus. Ye did improve considerably on yers, and I'd, of course, expect to improve on mine."

"And ye'd be a-saying so yerself," added their father, "if it wouldnae sound so like boasting and a-counting one's lambs before they've dropped."

There was a brief moment of uncomfortable silence.

"Aye, Father," said Duncan at last. "And I thank ye for the rebuke. I most heartily thank ye. And, brother, Angus," he went on extending his hand, "will ye forgive my pride? I am most ashamed of it."

Lindsay put her arm through Duncan's left arm and smiled up at him approvingly. The fumes seemed to begin clearing as Angus gripped his brother's hand.

"If ye kent my heart," began Angus, "ye'd ken the evil winds that were a-blowing there and how much I am in need of the same rebuke."

The soggy thudding sounds of hard backslapping on wet wool were followed along with some good-natured ribbing about muskets and bows.

"Now then," said their father. "When things get close in a battle and there's no time for firing muskets," he eyed them both; then, with a rasping sound of steel on steel, he drew his claymore, "it's claymores."

9 CLAYMORES!

Angus groaned. Duncan was a *man* with a claymore; Angus knew himself to be very much a boy with one. And *so* his father knew him to be.

"As worthy Captain John Paton has taught," continued his father, his graying red hair and beard now drenched and darkened by the rain, "our best deterrent to the murdering designs of Claverhouse and his bloody dragoons descending on our field worship"—He made a great sweep of the air with his claymore—"is arms." For a moment he studied the blade of his claymore as he turned the hilt with his wrist. "—I wish it were not so," he added with passionate wistfulness.

"But we must have armed men on the side of the Covenant," he continued, "who ken how to use their weapons. Lads, when all efforts for peace with wicked men—and I do mean *all* efforts," he paused, eyeing his sons and grandson meaningfully. "When *all* efforts have been exhausted, then, and only then, it is prudent to keep their wickedness in bounds with our strength, with our weapons."

Angus thought he saw in his father's peace-loving face a

resigned sadness, mixed with a sort of hopeful longing, but always tempered by a firm resolve forced on him by the unhappy necessity of the evil times. If his father's enemies only knew how much his father longed for peace, Angus mused, and how loyal and useful a subject he would be in a nation where justice thrived. If they only knew what he knew of his father, all would be very different—and they wouldn't need to use claymores on one another.

"Angus," said his father, holding the blade and extending the claymore, hilt first, to him.

Angus couldn't help frowning at the encircling steel basket hilt of the weapon. He gripped it reluctantly, in the same way a child who does not like snakes might pick one up when forced to prove his boyhood to the grinning faces watching the rite of passage.

Duncan's claymore whizzed through the air as he warmed to the practice bout with his little brother. Angus watched as Duncan stood on guard, feigned, parried, and lunged—at the falling rain. Angus tried to imitate the prebout antics of his brother, but his father's claymore felt heavy and clumsy in his hands. He felt rather ridiculous and glanced at his sister and nephew looking on through the rain.

"Now, hear me for the rules of engagement, lads," said their father, looking soberly first at Duncan, then Angus and back to Duncan again. "I want ye to fight with will and purpose, but I'll have no blood. Moreover, the first of ye who draws his brother's blood will face my blade—flat on his backside. Do ye understand, lads?"

"Aye, Father," they replied together.

"When I say 'halt,'" their father continued, "ye halt, midstroke and no further, understood?"

"Aye."

Duncan tried to grin in a reassuring manner as he brought

his blade up to his chin in salute. Angus returned the salute but not the grin.

"On yer guard, then, lads," said their father. "Commence fighting."

No sooner had the words left their father's lips, and Duncan feigned a lunge at Angus's middle. Angus attempted to block the thrust with a parry, but in his eagerness, and due to the weight of the blade, he overcompensated. Swinging his sword in a flourishing arc, Angus found himself hopelessly out of position and completely exposed to the cleaving stroke that would have followed but for the "Halt!" from his father.

Angus wiped dribbles of rain from his forehead and shifted his weight from one foot to the other. This was not going so well. He would have been dead within seconds had this been a real fight.

"Angus, ye must parry only as much as is needed to deflect the blow, like this," said his father, stepping behind him and moving Angus's sword arm in short, tight parries. "Otherwise, lad, ye leave yerself open to the next stroke—likely the last. Now, then, try again."

The next hour progressed in much the same manner: short bursts of fighting with frequent halts for guidance from his father. Angus calculated that had this been an hour of real fighting, he would have needed considerably more than nine lives to have survived. But no blood was drawn, and he had to admit that a glimmer of some of the theory behind the hacking, cutting ways of fighting with the claymore began to creep into his understanding. But he did not like it. And on the whole, it was a humiliating morning.

"That's enough for today, lads," his father said, none too soon for Angus.

"Ye, no doubt, have other strengths, brother," said Duncan, not unkindly, as he shook hands.

"Not forgetting, Duncan," said Jennie, her hair dripping around her face, "that ye had to learn the claymore sometime yerself, if I'm not mistaken."

"Aye, Duncan," said their father, "and I seem to remember considerable flailing and bumbling coming from yer blade in those days."

"'Tis all too true, too true," said Duncan, slapping Angus on the shoulder. "We'll be making a fighter of ye yet, that we will."

"But what of fighting with the bow?" blurted Angus. "I can hit my mark. I ken I can hit it."

"All right, I'll admit ye hit the bull's-eye," said Duncan. "But when the shooting part of battle is over, ye've got to be able to fight with the claymore."

"Why?" asked Angus as they made their way down the soggy moor to the warmth of their crofts.

"Why, ye ask?" said Duncan. "Well, it's just what's done in fighting."

"But that's all because it takes so long to load a musket," replied Angus, warming to the debate. "There'd be little need for claymores if ye could continue firing rapidly at yer enemy, now would there?"

Duncan looked at his brother as if he were from another world.

"Go on," said his father.

"We can make bows and arrows from all that we find right here on the moor," continued Angus, gesturing with his bow at the misty expanse. "And ye've both told me how at Rullion Green we Covenanters had only twenty pounds of gunpowder. Why? Because it's so expensive. And it's worthless when it gets wet—not so good a thing for Scotland. Arrows are easily made, easily retrieved, and easily reused. I ken I haven't shown it so well today, but I'm convinced the bow's more accurate than a musket. What's more, ye can shoot in the rain."

Duncan took a cut with his claymore at the wet moor grass.

"Ye're right. With muskets, we depend on volley fire," said Duncan. "I admit it. Ye just aim the thing in the general direction of the enemy's line and hope it fires. If most of ours fire—well, it's the combined effect of all that which does the damage."

"What?" asked Angus, not believing his ears.

"What Duncan says is true," said their father.

"But, then," stammered Angus. "Why not use the bow, then?"

"Aye, I'm thinking," replied Duncan, "that not just anybody can be taught to shoot like Angus, here." He ruffled Angus's dripping hair and put his arm across his brother's shoulder. "Shooting like that takes a special skill, a skill most of us'll never have."

Angus blinked rapidly and stared at his brother. Realization of Duncan's meaning sank in only slowly. Angus didn't trust himself to reply.

10 MURDER!

"Och, Angus, ye're going to rob me of my bishop!" cried Jennie later that night, May 2, 1679. She scowled at what remained of her half of the homemade chessmen. "Ye've got me hemmed in on all sides. How do ye do it?"

Angus did feel a twinge of remorse for even asking his sister to play chess with him. He still had to remind her that it was bishops not knights that moved diagonally. And then she often forgot that pawns only move forward. Though he had tried to teach her some of the strategies, some of the planning ahead that was so important to winning in chess, Jennie seemed unable to get beyond simply keeping the different pieces straight.

"Sorry, Jennie, but ye cannae move yer bishop like that," he said as kindly as he could. "And . . . well . . . Jennie, it's not yer turn."

"Och, brother." She threw her hands in the air and laughed. "Ye're a sight too clever for me. All right, then, finish me off. I'll cover my eyes, but do make it a clean stroke. And then, I'll teach ye to knit yer own socks. Fair trade, I should think."

"Two moves and ye're finished, Jennie."

"How can ye possibly ken that? Ye donnae ken just where

I'm going to move. I've a mind of my own, then. How could ye ken where I'll be moving next?"

"I fear it's none so hard as all that, Jennie. Ye've only two moves on the entire board."

"Has it come to that?"

"Show yer sister some mercy, Angus," said Duncan, looking at the board over his brother's shoulder.

"Och. That's just it. I've tried."

The rain had finally stopped falling in the early evening, the family had finished its dinner some time ago, and Sandy M'Kethe was just preparing to lead them in the worship of God. It sounded as if Angus would bring the chess game to its end any moment. As he rose to his feet and reached for his Bible, a sound outside the croft suddenly caught his ear.

"Checkmate, I fear, Jennie," said Angus, moving his queen with a plunk. Then he saw his father poised with his head cocked and his ears at full attention. "What is it, Father?"

"Horse," his father replied, covering the distance to the door in three strides.

Angus jumped to his feet and reached for his bow. His father snatched up his claymore and flung open the door. With thumping hooves and the rattling of harness, a lone horseman reined in his steed. The lathered and weary horse neighed and champed at its bit.

"It's the archbishop! The archbishop!" a breathless voice cried out in the dusky evening light.

"Oh, is it?" said Lindsay, looking down the path behind the horseman. "Stopping in for a pastoral visit, is he?"

"Dead!" the man cried again. "Archbishop Sharp, killed at Magus Moor for his crimes!"

"How killed?" asked Sandy M'Kethe steadily.

The man hesitated for an instant before replying. "If ye own the Covenant," said the man, "ye'll be grateful he's dead, man, and ask no more questions."

"How killed?" asked Angus's father insistently.

"He was in his fine carriage," began the man, haltingly.

"Go on."

"A-and men—loyal men, Covenant-keepers, all—" The horseman bit his lower lip, then blurted, "stopped the carriage and . . . killed him dead."

"What men?" asked Sandy M'Kethe, saying each word with care and restraint.

"James Russell, and others."

"Their leader?"

"John Burly Balfour, he laid and hatched the plot."

"And his foul deed will bring down on our heads, ours and the wee bairns here," said Mary M'Kethe with a moan, "the fury of the king."

"Fiona, we'll gather the twins and go inside," said Jamie, lifting a three-year-old under each arm. "Shall Papa be telling ye a story?"

"Aye, the one about slaying the giant," said little Sandy eagerly.

"All right, then," said their father as the little family disappeared into the croft.

"When did it happen?" asked Sandy M'Kethe of the horseman.

" 'Twas nigh on noon, today."

"And just how did it come about, then?"

"His fancy state-coach, drawn by six of the finest horses, was returning the foul persecutor of the Kirk to his seat in St.

Andrews from the Privy Counsel meeting—his last. His final act, fitting of his bloody career, was his drafting a proclamation—found in the coach after the noble deed was accomplished—empowering almost anyone as agent of the Crown to seize, try, and execute on the spot any Covenanter suspected of carrying arms at a conventicle."

"Go on."

"Burly Balfour and his fellows, nine in all, headed off the coach with pistol fire and naked blades. Sharp, that Judas of the Kirk, screamed at his coachman, 'Drive, drive!' says he. But Balfour and his men cut the harness and traces, and hamstrung the leading horse. They dragged out the traitor, who fell to his knees and begged for the life of his daughter."

"His daughter?"

"Aye, his daughter. Sharp begged for her life—which the noble executioners spared, though she was wounded."

"Foul indeed," said Sandy M'Kethe, shaking now with anger as he reconstructed the scene in his mind.

"Aye, he was, but he's with the devil now."

"Ye mistake my meaning, man. Carry on with yer tale of woe."

"Balfour refused to hear the slobbering entreaties of the brute who never showed pity to any man, and he gave him a cut to the head."

"Ye mean he lifted his sword against an unarmed man, and without a fair trial?"

"Nae, nae. They tried him in the episcopal way right on the moor—after the fashion of his own proclamation. And he *was* armed. The coach fairly bristled with pistols and shot. Whereupon, the nine fell to ending his miserable life with claymore, dagger, and pistol—a wound for each of the liberators, so I'm told."

"And his daughter saw it all," said Sandy M'Kethe in a

listless tone, his eyes sad and gazing into the darkness as he spoke.

"Aye, as I'm told."

"Do ye have any bairns, man? A daughter, perhaps?"

The horseman blinked and swallowed several times before answering.

"Aye."

" 'Tis a most foul, murdering deed."

"I'm just delivering the message," said the horseman. "I thought this might do good for the Covenanting cause, then," he added lamely.

"I have no love for Sharp's murdering ways," said Sandy M'Kethe. "And he surely was the chief designer of our woes. But murder's murder. And there's no justice in it. With this foul deed, these men bring more harm to the Covenant than any of us kens."

"But, man," retorted the horseman, returning to his original enthusiasm. "Sharp *was* the chief cause of all our woe. Now he lies in his own blood near St. Andrew's dead—gone—finished." The man's horse shied and pranced sideways. " 'Tis a great victory for the Covenant. And here ye are, ungrateful and quibbling about whether it was murder or a just killing, then."

"Anyone who takes obedience to the Law of God seriously," replied Sandy M'Kethe, "must quibble, as ye call it, about what's good and what's evil. This deed is evil. And, O, alas, may our bairns be spared of the paying for it."

With a huff, the man yanked on his reins, turned, and galloped down the moor.

"What happens next, Father?" asked Angus as they turned and went back inside.

His father barred the door with care but did not reply immediately. He reached for his big Bible and slumped wearily onto a chair near the hearth and across from where his wife always sat in the evenings. She picked up her knitting and, in a flurry, the woody clicking of knitting needles and the quavering humming of the tune "Martyrs" rose from her corner. Jennie, Fiona, and Lindsay joined her, and in a moment the corner of the room fairly hummed with the rhythm of their knitting.

Malcolm sat wide-eyed on his father's knee, and the twins lolled blissfully near the hearth talking in a three-year-old manner to each other through the persona of little wool dolls that their grandmother had made for them.

"A most bad, bad man," said little Sandy, turning his doll's head side to side.

"Aye, bad, bad," agreed little Mary's doll, jumping up and down for emphasis with each word.

"But now he's dead," said little Sandy's doll.

"Aye, he's dead, dead," replied little Mary's doll, "just like Goliath."

"And they all lived happily ever after," said Sandy's doll, nodding with finality.

"Ever, ever after," agreed Mary's doll.

Tears welled up in Mary M'Kethe's eyes as she listened to the children's talk. "Oh, if God would but spare the wee ones." She dropped her knitting and took up the twins on her lap. They squirmed under her strong embrace. "There was a day when I would have rejoiced at just such news as we have heard," she said. "And I'd hae thought much the same as these wee ones about it all."

"But there's no cause for rejoicing in this news," said her husband. "Balfour and his hot-headed murderers acted foolishly. And I fear that that foolish deed will bring no happy end to our woes. Aye, as the wisest man once wrote, 'Wisdom is better than weapons of war, but one sinner destroys much good.' I fear Balfour, preferring bloody weapons over wisdom, has gone and besmirched the cause of the Covenant. And we all, alas, must pay for his folly."

"But would it hae made any difference," said Jamie, gazing pensively into the fire, "if Sharp had been on his way to order the death of Mr. Douglas or Mr. Peden, or maybe to stop a field meeting by shooting the minister and anyone in arms who resisted. Would it still hae been murder, then, Father?"

"Aye, does he hae to be in the very act of killing," said Angus, "for our stopping him to be self-defense, and, thus, a just killing?"

"But, if what the messenger said was true," added Duncan, "Sharp actually *was* in the act of seeing to our death. With that proclamation, all of us would be lawbreakers and subject to death—on the spot. I donnae like the bit about the daughter, but might stopping the evil man hae been justified, for all the lives it saves?"

"Och, Duncan, that's the devil's reasoning," said their father. "To scheme and plot for a man's life, no matter how evil the man"—he passed a heavy hand across his brow—"that's the lying-in-wait kind of killing. Murder, it is, lads, and make no mistake."

"But did not Sharp deserve to die?" said Lindsay as she tenderly braided Mary's red locks.

"Aye," agreed Jennie, her needles silent. "No one man in all Scotland has heaped more evil on the faithful than Sharp, I'm sure of it."

"As am I," said Sandy M'Kethe. "Aye, he deserved to die, Lindsay. But our sins being what they are, we must see justice done within the sure boundaries of law and order—law and order based on God's Law."

"But Sharp's laws," said Angus, "were not based on God's Law."

"I ken the king's laws," said Lindsay, a faraway sadness in her gaze. "My father kent the king's laws. There's nothing of God's Law in them."

"Aye, but that's no justification for us to act outside of the law," said Sandy M'Kethe. "Ye cannae fix injustice—with more of it."

For several moments no one said anything.

"So, what happens next?" asked Angus, giving words to what nearly everyone in the room was thinking.

"If God doesnae see fit to deliver us," said Mary M'Kethe, her voice quavering with emotion, "Lauderdale'll send out bloody Claverhouse and more dragoons with still more license to wreak a smoking vengeance on all Ayrshire. I should think the Highland barbarians will be unleashed to still greater mischief, as well."

"I pity the Whytes," said Jennie.

"Aye, and Willy," said Angus, his jaw tensing. "What do we do, Father?"

His father smiled. "We pray."

"And we obey," joined Angus, in chorus with his father's familiar words.

"And the Sabbath," continued Angus. "Do we go to worship God at the trysting place on the Sabbath?"

"The prophet Daniel didnae stop praying for fear of envious men who sought his life," his father replied, his tone resolved and firm. He reached out and took up his wife's cold hands in his, squeezing them reassuringly. "And nor shall we."

"But, O, I fear," said his wife, "we'll all hang for Burly Balfour's crimes."

11 UISGE BEATHA

Lurid details of the murder and aftermath flooded like a torrent throughout the region over the next days. Burly Balfour and his assassins were on the run and hounded on every side by Claverhouse and the king's dragoons. Most agreed that it seemed somehow appropriate that Bishop Paterson, notorious inventor of the thumbscrew, a torture device used liberally on captured Covenanters, preached Sharp's funeral sermon. When the sermon ended Sharp was a martyr on the level of Stephen.

Foremost in almost every conversation from St. Andrew's to Dalry was the question, "Was Sharp's death a matter of justice—or was it murder?" Royalists knew the answer, and soldiers of the Crown were on the move to avenge the murder; reports of violence and death mounted daily.

The night of the murder, young Andrew Ayton of Inchdarnie, while riding peacefully in the woods near Magus Moor—Bible in hand and on his way to hear a preacher at Cupar—was summarily shot and killed by a party of soldiers. Reportedly, the "comely sweet youth" was no older than Angus.

Two days after the murder, the Sabbath dawned. Throughout Fife, Lanarkshire, Mid Lothian Scotland, Ayrshire, and beyond, the king's dragoons lustily readied their horses and their weapons. Highlanders quartered in the Irvine valley below the M'Kethe ferm-toun had been stirred into a frenzy of expectancy for a Sabbath of plunder—and of killing.

"We'll not forsake the assembling of ourselves," said Sandy M'Kethe, meanwhile, to his little clan. Everyone was scrubbed, dressed, and ready for the tramp down the valley and up to the trysting place.

"But, Father, with all that is astir," began Duncan, glancing nervously at Lindsay coddling his twins on her lap. "Do ye think it wise to venture out?"

"Aye, the Holy Book tells us not to forsake assembling ourselves together, and all the more—*all the more*, lad—as we see the Day of the Lord approaching. This would be one of those days where we see the Day of the Lord approaching. We'll venture forth in obedience to our Redeemer and render praise and worship to him with the saints. And though I intend to trust our safety into his all powerful hands—we shall be prudent."

The late archbishop's proclamation against Covenanters carrying arms, notwithstanding, along with Bible and Psalter, Sandy M'Kethe, Duncan, and Jamie each carried musket and claymore. Angus shouldered his bow.

Their father arranged the women and the children, who fidgeted with a mixture of dread and anticipation of the day's dangers, in a defensible cluster.

"Duncan, Jamie, ye'll fan out on our flank and be at the ready for the worst. I'll plant myself in the lead. Mind ye, lads, keep yer match cord glowing and yer powder dry."

Flinch stood preening on Angus's shoulder, his coal-black feathers shimmering in the morning sunlight; he strutted and bobbed, admiring himself. Angus racked his brain trying to think of some possible advantage to bringing Flinch along for the day. What had William Cleland said? "Ye'd see Highlanders' heels if they heard Flinch talk."

"King and Kirk! King and Kirk!" screeched the crow.

Angus groaned. But how could he be sure?

"Flinch stays, Angus," said his father. "If ye'd taught it to say, 'Big are bishops, big are bishops,' or some such nonsense, I might allow it to come. But with that stock it'd expose us for sure."

Flinch did his best imitation of the cooing of a pigeon as Angus put the bird within the sod walls of the family dovecote.

"Now, then, let us commit our way unto the Lord," said Sandy M'Kethe when Angus rejoined them. They sang together:

> Judge me, O God, and plead my cause
>   Against th'ungodly nation . . .
>
> O send thy light forth and thy truth;
>   Let them be guides to me,
> And bring me to thine holy hill,
>   Ev'n where thy dwellings be.
>
> Then will I to God's altar go,
>   To God my chiefest joy . . .

When they finished singing, Sandy M'Kethe said, "Now, then, we go forth in the Lord's strength."

"Uh . . . Father," began Angus, shifting from one foot to the other.

"O, I've not forgotten ye, lad," he said, placing a big hand on his son's shoulder.

"Angus, yer bow may aid us more than ye ken," he said. "Carry it like a walking stick and keep yer arrows covered well under yer plaid, there. Ye'll act as our scout. Go on ahead. Keep us in yer sight, and signal us to halt and scatter if ye see anything amiss. And, Angus, do remember the shortness of the wee bairns' legs."

Angus grinned, and without a word he turned and headed down the moor.

"To Loudoun Hill then," said his father. "And keep a keen eye, lad," he called.

"And no poetry!" called Duncan.

***

Half an hour later, Angus lay hidden in the moor grass, scanning the Irvine valley for any sign of Highlanders on the move, or for the glint of sunlight on the helmets or weapons of a troop of horse. The most treacherous part of the morning's journey lay just below. Nowhere else would they be so exposed to sight as when crossing through the valley, and over the well-traveled road to Edinburgh that snaked away to the east.

To the north rose the bulging bulwark of Loudoun Hill, the sunlight warm on the rocky fells of its southwest face, the shadows deepening the green terraces of the gentler east-facing slopes. If they could just traverse the base of the hill around to the north where others would be gathering to hear the preaching of Mr. John King, and where the hill itself would block them from prying eyes lurking along the road. But first, they had to cross the valley.

Like when sheep grow twitchy and restless before a storm, a skittering uneasiness came over Angus. He glanced behind through the grass. His father's graying hair appeared first. Next, Angus could see his father's alert eyes moving side to side, searching for any sign of trouble. The rest followed close on his heels. Angus looked again at the valley.

Then he saw them.

A mob of fifteen or twenty Highlanders, kilted in earthy tartans, walked in a spread-out disorderly phalanx. They carried muskets, and as near as he could tell, each man wore a claymore at his hip. The clan chief out in front wore a pheasant feather in his blue bonnet, a long, horse-hair sporran bounced from his waist, and he seemed altogether more alert than the rest.

So close was Angus that he heard some of them talking. One threw back his shaggy head and attempted to sing. Another paused and lifted a drinking flask to his lips. Then, in obvious disgust, he held the empty flask upside down and shook it wildly. Nothing came out.

"Tha mi!" Angus heard the man yell. He sifted through his memory, trying to remember the little Gaelic he'd picked up along the way.

"Tha mi ag iarraidh—uisge beatha," the man cried.

He wants what? Angus thought, bewildered, as he looked down at the drunken Highlander holding his empty flask.

"O, uisge beatha! Uisge beatha!" the man wailed.

Then, in disgust, it occurred to Angus: the man wants uisge beatha—the water of life, as the Gaelic had it; or just uisge—whiskey, in Scot's English.

Suddenly, it seemed that one of the Highlanders looked up the moor. Angus's heart pounded wildly against the springy heather, and he glanced frantically behind for his family. His father would not yet be able to see the Highlanders, blocked from sight as they were by the knoll where Angus lay hidden. His pulse pounded like the thundering of kettledrums before a battle, and he wondered if the Highlanders might hear it. In a matter of four or five strides, his father would come into full view, and if any one of those men traipsing through the valley happened to be looking up the moor then, his father and family would all be discovered. *Fine scout I make*, he thought bitterly. Worse yet, if Angus now rose and gave warning, he would be immediately heard and seen—and all would be lost.

Suddenly a thought struck. The Highlanders wouldn't see or hear an arrow—and his father would. But he had to work fast. Rolling on his side, he wrenched his bow around his leg and set his teeth as he strained the bowstring in place. It was harder stringing a bow lying down. Next, he flung his plaid aside, grabbed an arrow, set it on the string, took one last glance at the Highlanders, and at where his father and family walked, drew the string and let fly into the clouds. Fearful that his father might have been looking the other way, without pausing he set another arrow on the string and shot it off to the left side of where he'd last seen his family—walking into dangers they knew nothing of. Then he waited.

Let them see it, O Lord, please let them see the arrows, cried Angus inwardly.

But he was almost afraid to look at the valley. Had the Highlanders seen his arrows—instead of his father?

He glanced back at where he'd last seen his family. Nothing. It was if they had never been there. It had worked. He imagined Malcolm and the twins huddled in the heather, their mother's arms clutching protectively over them. And he imagined his father and Duncan and Jamie lying on their bellies, puffing gently on their match cord ready to fire if absolutely necessary. Through the moor grass, he watched as the clan chief scanned the surrounding hills, then signaled his men eastward. Within moments, they disappeared around a bend. Angus expelled his breath in a great puffing sigh. Stealing one last look around, he rose cautiously to his feet and, in a bent-over run, streaked back toward his family.

"Ye didnae give us any too much room to spare, lad," said his father as Angus joined the family.

"Fifteen or twenty Highlanders, heading due east through the valley," he gasped. "I donnae think they saw us, praise be to God."

"I cannae bear to think what they would hae done to the wee ones," Angus heard his mother say as she gripped her husband's arm, "if we'd fallen into the hands of such wild creatures."

"Aye, but we're not in their hands, Mary, m'love," he said patting her hand reassuringly. "We're in the Lord's."

Angus looked at Jennie. A stray lock of her auburn hair swirled in the breeze. She tucked it aside and smoothed her hands nervously on her dress. The color drained from her cheeks, and a haunting presentiment flickered in her eyes.

Squeezing her hand, Angus whispered, "Come what may, Jennie, I'd do all I could to make certain no harm came to ye."

"This next bit is the worst," said their father. "It behooves us to be most cautious. We'll cross the Edinburgh road in twos and threes, and gather again at the base of Loudoun Hill, just there." He pointed to a clump of short Scots pine across the valley. "Angus, lead the way."

12 HILLTOP SENTINEL

"He hands nations over to him
And subdues kings before him.
He turns them to dust with his sword,
To windblown chaff with his bow."

From where Angus lay on a warm slab of rock at the summit of Loudoun Hill, he strained to hear. When the breeze blew gently and from the north, it carried bits and pieces of Mr. John King's words as he read from the prophet Isaiah and chapter forty-one. Even from a distance, Angus caught the lilting passion and the blood-firing authority ringing in the fugitive minister's voice as he read from the ancient poetry. Glad as Angus was to stand as one of the sentries for the field meeting—painful experience had taught Covenanters to always, *always* enlist sharp-eyed and armed sentries during field worship—nevertheless, as he caught snatches of the service, he longed to hear all and join in the sacred rites.

". . . Ye, O Israel . . . Jacob, whom I have chosen . . .
Ye are my servant; I have chosen ye . . ."

A thrill shivered down Angus's neck and spine as the minister's voice wafted to his rocky post. He shook his head to clear it, reached for his bow, and with eyes narrowed, he scanned the undulating waves of green fields, flecked with spots of wooly foam, surrounding the hill. To the northeast a ridge of stone rose on the horizon two miles away—Drumclog, the ancients had named it.

Angus looked over the rocky fells of the hill and imagined himself a long-ago sentry of Robert the Bruce. It was 1307, and the Bruce with his little band of freedom fighters arrayed themselves at the base of the hill, determined to drive back the masses of King Edward's cavalry. By sheer numbers things looked hopeless for Scotland, but Bruce had a plan. As Angus recollected the story, Bruce had ordered his men to dig pits down there and cover them over. When the heavy English cavalry thundered toward the fledgling Scots army, they plunged into the concealed pits. At the end of the day, the battlefield was heaped with crumpled mounds of horseflesh and the broken remains of English knights. Scotland had won.

He tore his eyes away from the ancient battlefield. It wouldn't do for a sentry to be caught daydreaming about past victory. Moving his eyes westward, he watched patches of sunlight glittering where the River Irvine emptied into the Firth of Clyde eight miles away. Beyond stretched the open sea. And just visible on the blue water were the square-rigged sails of one of the king's ships scudding down the coast patrolling for smugglers. The king's Counsel in Edinburgh had ordered coastal patrols to ensure that no Covenanter be allowed to flee to Holland—or to the American colonies.

For a moment Angus imagined himself in the crow's nest of a mighty sailing ship. He'd read a good deal about

Loudoun Hill

sea battles and voyages in the earl's books. His task: to search the high seas for enemy sail, and then give out the alarm to heave-to for the fight. As the white and gray of the clouds scudded overhead, the sun winking through and flooding the briny green with shafts of gold, imagining the hill to move with the waves like a ship—became easier and easier.

Again the wind carried Mr. King's voice so he could hear it clearly.

> ". . . Do not fear, for I am with ye
>   Do not be dismayed, for I am yer God.
> I will strengthen ye and help ye . . ."

With these words, Angus took another sweep with his eyes at the fields—and at the road stretching away to Edinburgh, and to the king's bloody Privy Counsel, the blaspheming Court of High Commission, and the garrison of thieving dragoons. West on the same road lay Glasgow with its ancient cathedral and drunken bishop, and carousing between all, along with the thieving Highlanders, lurked vicious John Graham of Claverhouse and his brutal troop of horse. And, what with avenging the murder of Sharp, the entire force of the Covenant-breaking King Charles II hieing at their heels, hungry for blood.

Perhaps brought on by his close encounter with Highlanders that morning, Angus felt a creeping bitterness deep within his heart. *Twang*. Brooding, he strummed his bowstring. *Twang, twang*. And then words began forming in his mind, words given shape by a constant theological and aesthetic diet of Hebrew poetry. Opening his pouch, he pulled out his roll of paper and a bit of charcoal. Frowning at the world in general, he wrote:

Like madmen they in ambush wait
To pierce us through with rage and hate.
Their brazen plan, a brutal snare:
Does God not see, nor hear, nor care?

Mr. King's voice, aided by the breeze, again broke in on his muse.

> ". . . Those who oppose ye will be as nothing and
> perish.
> Those who wage war with ye will be as nothing at all."

Is this just metaphor? Angus wondered bitterly, searching the horizon for any glint of steel or fluttering of banner, for the hellish spurring of Claverhouse and his brigade of leering dragoons. For long grinding years those faithful to the Covenant had brutally suffered. *Maybe they've had things all turned around,* Angus wondered. After all, it was Covenanters who were doing the perishing; Covenanters were the ones coming to nothing. The minister's voice rose to a crescendo:

> "For I am the Lord, yer God,
> Who takes hold of yer right hand
> And says to ye, Do not fear;
> I will help ye."

The wind shifted and the minister's words became indistinct. All that reached his ears now was the occasional wailing of a hungry infant, a loud sneeze, the clink of steel, the clearing of a raspy throat, the snorting of a horse, and the rattle of harness.

Resolving to scan the surrounding countryside at regular

intervals, Angus reached for the earl's book. Finding his place, he read:

> . . . and let us consider, again, that all the law is not in the hands of Giant Despair: others, so far as I can understand, have been taken by him as well as we; and yet have escaped out of his hand: Who knows, but that God who made the world, may cause that Giant Despair may die; or that at some time he may forget to lock us in . . . for my part I am resolved to pluck up the heart of a man, and to try my utmost to get from under his hand . . .

He paused, scanning carefully the surrounding hills and fields. *Others . . . have escaped out of his hand.* And then, like a flood, Angus thought of Moses, of Joseph, of David, of Daniel, of Elijah. *Pluck up the heart of a man. Do not fear; I will help ye . . . God who made the world . . .* He felt a thrill of hope wash over him.

And just when all seemed well again, his blood ran cold. Off in the distance four mounted men galloped east on the road. No redcoats; no glint of armored helm or breastplate. Not Highlanders. He frowned, wishing he could see who they were. No sense in sounding an alarm until he could be certain they posed a threat.

"Ye're stiff as a cat, Angus M'Kethe," William Cleland's voice startled him. William flopped down beside Angus and followed his gaze. "Och, what have we here, then?"

"I donnae ken," said Angus in a whisper, though more than a mile separated the horsemen from them. "But, look! They're leaving the road."

"Aye, and making their way direct toward us."

"Who are they?" asked Angus.

"Too far to say," said William, rolling on his side and

checking his musket. "But I intend to be ready for them. Now, be off with ye, Angus. I'm to relieve ye of duty now anyway. Ye'd best sound the alarm so the men can stand ready."

Angus scrambled to his feet, grabbed up his book and bow, and ran to the edge of the hilltop. Plunging down the steep grassy slope, terraced by meandering sheep paths, he tried to calculate how much time before the horsemen would arrive. It required considerable concentration not to miscalculate his step with all those sheep tracks crisscrossing the steepness. People came in sight, and they all seemed to be looking his way. He later remembered the open-mouthed astonishment on their faces—and how it turned to mirth.

But at just that moment, Angus found the sloping ground not at all where he thought it should be. Too fast. And too steep. Then in a rolling, bouncing, skiddering tumble, he found himself gaining more and more speed—finally losing all control. Over and over he fell.

To the band of worshipers, prayers were suddenly interrupted by a whirling ball of plaid and black hair, a ball with arms groping the air and feet desperately splayed out for footing. Scattered arrows and a bow strewed the hillside behind it. At the base of the hill, the ball dissolved into a rumpled heap of boy as Angus came to rest at the feet of the fugitive minister, Mr. King.

"Is this, lad, yer act of worship, then?" said the minister, a smile playing at the corners of his mouth. "Ah, perhaps it's some late revision to Laud's Liturgy."

"Are ye hurt, Angus?" he heard his mother's voice and felt her hand stroking his brow.

He struggled to his feet, aided by his mother and several others. Caught in his clothes and hair were tufts of grass and sprigs of heather, and stray bits of damp wool clung to his hair.

"Four men of horse approaching from the south," he gasped, his cheeks hot and red from more than the battering descent.

"Claverhouse?" one man demanded.

"No."

"Redcoats?" another man demanded.

"No."

"Highlanders?" demanded another.

"No."

"Armed?" this from his father.

"They carried arms," replied Angus. "And William Cleland watches from the hill."

Many voices rose, all speaking at the same time.

"Four against all of us," he heard one man say. While another added, "If they come in hostility, they donnae stand a prayer against us."

While they spoke the sliding of ramrods joined the noise as men primed muskets and readied pistols for defense. In minutes the men formed a circle around the women and children—some moaning and sobbing. One row of men stood and another knelt in front, muskets and claymores at the ready. Sandy M'Kethe, Duncan, and Jamie formed a wall of protection around their women and children. As Angus gathered up his bow and arrows from the hillside, he heard Mr. King's voice rise above them all.

"The God of Jacob is our refuge, dear people. He holds ye by yer right hand. Have no fear. Put yer hope in God."

And then, from around a buttress at the base of the hill, four men came suddenly into view, reining in their horses from a full gallop.

"Put down yer weapons," called the leader. "We come in peace." A thickset man dismounted and strode confidently toward the encircled worshipers.

Angus studied the man's face. There was something about his smile. It seemed too wide, and his mouth curled down instead of up. His face was broad, and he wore a bonnet high on his head, exposing a wide forehead. The hard line of his eyebrows shielded dark, close-set eyes, and his thin straight nose seemed to stand as a sharp divide on his face.

"John Burly Balfour," said one man, lowering his gun.

The faces of the worshipers betrayed mixed feelings about the newcomer. Not all the men lowered their guns.

"Balfour and his minions, that is," said one bitterly.

"No murderer has a part in the Kingdom of God," said another.

"Aye, and I've just freed ye from such a murderer," retorted Balfour. "And, mind ye, it were no murder delivering God's people from the likes of Sharp."

"That will be finally known on the Great Day," said Mr. King. "We trust ye had good intentions, man. But the road to hell is made wide and broad with just such intentions, when those intentions are not sanctified by justice born of wise counsel."

Balfour's eyes grew darker, but he made no reply.

"We must be united in defense of religious liberty," said Sandy M'Kethe, "and the cause of the weak. Brutally murdering a man—even such a man as Sharp—in full view of his daughter, and wounding her in the bargain, man! Ye've only brought down on all our heads the unmitigated wrath of the king and of Claverhouse, who even now may be trampling these hills, wreaking the vengeance of yer foul deed—on these." His hand swept meaningfully over the huddle of women and children.

"I'm tempted, Mr. King," said Balfour, turning his back on Angus's father, "to hear in yer words the ring of the Indulged clergy, so I am. Ye sound to me as if ye want peace with episcopacy." He spat out the word, then snorted in derision. "Ye'll only come by that peace by joining the Indulged betrayers of the Covenant. And when ye do that ye become—our enemy."

"Mr. King has sworn no oath of allegiance to the king in matters of the Kirk," said the earl of Loudoun, stepping forward and standing between the minister and Balfour. "And he's made no compromise with episcopacy. He lives the life of a fugitive and daily risks that life for the spiritual well-being of his scattered flock, and he ranks among the best of preachers for his love of truth and his proclamation of grace and redemption."

"Ye're correct that I long for peace in Christ's troubled Kirk, man," said Mr. King. "But not at the expense of her purity. I've betrayed no Covenant made with God or man, nor am I ranked among the Indulged clergy of Scotland. But, we must be slow to hack off our own limbs. I grieve to see the hatred of the faithful toward those misguided ministers who have seen fit to join the Indulged and keep their pulpits. I do long for peace and unity among brothers, but that doesnae make me Indulged."

Here Balfour turned his narrowed eyes on the earl of Loudoun.

"And what of yer continued association with the likes of the Marquess of Douglas and other lairds who pay the cess. If ye donnae condemn them, ye become a partaker of their evil betrayal."

"The cess tax is a cruel means cooked up by the king," said the earl, his jaw working as he restrained his anger. "By it faithful lairds find themselves heavily taxed to fund the garrisons of dragoons that pillage their own people and lands."

"And if they pay the cess," interrupted Balfour, "they betray those same people."

"So it might seem to ye, sir," said the earl, barely able to keep his voice steady.

"There cannae be any other way to see it, man."

"I hae never paid a farthing of cess tax, and ye may ask any man to confirm my words. But I will not go, as Mr. King has it, hacking off my brothers whose trials and woe may be greater than my own. I hate the cess, but I'll not stoop to hating those who feel compelled to pay it."

"Amen and amen!" shouted many, but not all.

"Well, donnae let me interrupt worship," said Balfour, casting his eyes over the gathering. "I see ye've prepared the Lord's Table here in the wilderness. I long to partake of it, that I do."

The man's last words sounded almost like a challenge. Angus looked at Mr. King. Would he let Balfour, the murderer of Sharp, partake?

Mr. King nodded to John Campbell, Earl of Loudoun, to Sir Robert Hamilton, to John Nisbet, to Thomas Fleming, and to Angus's father and several other men in the congregation, and while a psalm was sung, the elders of the congregation withdrew to deliberate. Angus stepped closer in hopes of hearing what they said. He only caught snatches over the psalm.

"He comes confessing Christ," said one, "he partakes."

"He comes disobeying Christ," said another, "and betraying his confession. We must fence him from the table. I see no other way."

"The bread and wine, symbols of Christ's body and blood," said another, "are *for* sinners. So they must be for Balfour."

"*Repentant* sinners, that is. And I donnae detect much that looks like true repentance in the man."

"But if he says the words, isnnae that enough?"

"Men, if we allow Balfour to partake," said Mr. King, "who would we ever bar? If we allow a murderer unconfessed to partake, we allow him to eat and drink in an unworthy manner, and bring down on his soul and ours God's ire."

"I move," said Sandy M'Kethe, "that we fence Balfour from the table. I believe we make trivial the precious body and blood of our gracious Redeemer to do otherwise."

"I second," said the earl.

The men cast their votes, and Balfour was barred from the Supper.

Fuming, almost threatening, Balfour and his men rode off.

When the supper ended and families were sent prayerfully on their way home, Angus and the men in his family talked briefly with the earl and William Cleland before making their way up the moor.

"I fear that reparations from the king," said the earl, "for Balfour's foul deed will be swift and bloody. We must have a plan. I only wish we had with us the likes of holy Richard Cameron and the valiant exiles in Holland who study and wait."

"Sir Robert Hamilton believes the time has come for us to make a stand," said Cleland. "And I cannae help believing he's right, though I too would rather make that stand with the likes of Cameron."

"We must defend the weak and the poor," said the earl. "That much is clear. And whatever it takes to do it, we must do." He paused and looked at Angus for a moment. "I donnae want to tell ye this, Angus."

"Tell me what?"

"Ye ken the Highlanders?" began the earl.

"I ken what they do."

"It's the Whytes," continued the earl. "The Highlanders have quartered themselves on the Whytes."

Angus's mouth went dry. What could they possibly hope to gain from a poor old couple—and from Willy?

"I will do all I can," continued the earl.

"What will become of Willy?" asked Angus, feeling a rising in his blood that he could not explain.

"We commend him to our Redeemer . . . and pray for his safety."

"But Highlanders," said Angus. Then a thought occurred to him, and the seed of a plan began forming in his mind. "These Highlanders . . . do ye ken if their clan chief is the one that . . . plays chess?"

"Aye, I believe it is," said the earl, looking sideways at Angus. "He's rarely beaten, and, I might just add, it hardly seems appropriate in times like these for ye, lad, to be thinking of chess."

"Aye, yer lairdship," said Angus. "I'll bear it in mind. I will bear it in mind."

13 THE DILEMMA

"Father, we must come to their aid," said Angus as they neared their ferm-toun on the moor.

Sabbath worship and the long trek from Loudoun Hill to their home nearly behind them, they made their last steps of the day in weary silence. But not Angus. His mind raced with the scenario of danger that even that moment might threaten the safety of his friends—especially Willy.

"Aye, lad," said his father. "I've thought of little else. But I confess every plan I consider ends in disaster. How to deliver them peacefully?" He wiped his brow and ran his fingers through the waves of his beard. "We confront a mob of Highlanders with our few weapons, and we're like to bring considerably more trouble on the Whytes—and on our own weak ones. I cannae see my way clearly on anything."

Weary from the long journey, Duncan and Jamie—children in arms—took their families to their own crofts for the night, while Angus and Jennie followed their parents into the M'Kethe cottage. Angus arranged peat on the grate as his father blew gently on the embers until they glowed red. Jennie and her mother prepared the evening meal.

"I hate the thought of one of those cowardly persecutors," said Angus's mother, pausing while slicing cheese, "wearing my socks." She wagged her knife for emphasis with each word.

"Aye, and the poor Whytes are sure to be going hungry," said Jennie as she set trenchers on the trestle table. "We must bring them food as we always do."

"But, Jennie, with Highland men sucking them dry," said their mother, "any food we bring will be snatched from their gums by the cruel monsters."

"We must try to help," continued Jennie. "More than ever they need our help."

"Oh, make no mistake," said their mother. "I'm all for helping. We can do nothing less, but how to do it? That is the question."

"Father, what do the Highlanders do during the day?" asked Angus. "I ken they eat all they can find, steal anything of value, and turn the Whytes out of their beds at night, but what do they do during the daytime?"

"Drink, I fear," said his father.

"Where?"

"I suppose they drink at the inn," he replied, frowning thoughtfully. "Or out on the hillside, or along the banks of the Irvine. What are ye getting at, Angus?"

"I could sneak down the south bank of the river in the forest," began Angus, excitement growing in his voice. "I'd watch the cottage, and when all's clear I could tend to the needs of the aged and Willy. Oh, Father, do let me go."

"Ye tend to their needs?" said Jennie. "Now, Angus, there are things ye do well and things I do well. If ye're going, I must be the one to go along and tend to their needs. I could clean up the cottage—it's no doubt in shambles. The Whytes might be sick—or injured. Oh, please, Father, let me go, too?"

Sandy M'Kethe looked at his daughter's pleading eyes. Like her mother, she grew all the more attractive when love for others animated her delicate features. She was like a red rose, subtle and intricate in beauty, compelling and evocative in her purity, and, like a rose—so easily destroyed. He shuddered and passed a callused hand over his brow. The hazard posed by his daughter's beauty haunted his mind. The color drained from his cheeks, and he felt cruel hands groping at his heart.

"Father, ye ken I'd stop at nothing," said Angus, eyeing his father, and slowly grasping the cause of the fear that clouded his father's eyes. "I'd do anything to guard Jennie from harm."

"Guard me?" said Jennie with a little laugh. "It's the Whytes we're trying to protect, here. And I can help. Oh, please, Father?"

"They'll be needing fresh bread and oatcakes," said their mother, taking down a basket and pursing her lips as she warmed to her usual pitch of generosity. She hummed the psalm tune "Dundee" as she worked.

"I donnae ken," said Sandy M'Kethe, an involuntary quaver in his voice. "If ye did stumble upon Highlanders . . ." He stared, unblinking, into the hissing glow of the fire, his eyes seeing things he would do anything to avoid. But his dear neighbors—poor, old, and weak—needed his help. Zeal for true and undefiled religion compelled him—if only there weren't the lustful Highlanders to fear.

"Why are these Highlanders so cruel?" asked Angus, feeling the heat rise in his face. "Are they sired by demons? I donnae understand what makes them such brute beasts to prey on we Lowlanders—even the weak and elderly. I'm half tempted to think they're more depraved than we."

His father's eyes flashed, and he reached for his Bible.

"There's none righteous, lad, leastwise those who think themselves more wise or deserving than their neighbors."

Angus swallowed but could make no reply.

"Paul tells the proud Corinthian Christians to 'think of what ye were when ye were called. Not many of ye were wise by human standards; not many were influential; not many were of noble birth'—though we have our lairds and ladies in the Kirk—'But God chose the foolish things of the world to shame the wise'—that is, God chose those who kent themselves to be foolish, to shame those who thought themselves to be the wise ones—'God chose the weak things of the world'—that'd be us, my dear ones—'to shame the strong,' those who think they're strong in themselves. St. Paul goes on and tells us that God chose the lowly things, the despised things, the things that are not 'to nullify the things that are, so that no one will boast.' No, my dear lad, Angus, we believe in Christ the King and Redeemer of his Kirk because he ordained us to believe from before the foundations of the world and not because we're more deserving than Highlanders. Never think that, lad, never."

"Thank ye," said Angus when he trusted himself to speak. "I'm so grateful for ye, Father—and for ye reminding me—again."

"A reminder we all need more often than we ken," said his father. "It does help to remember the darkness and superstition under which so many Highlanders live," he continued. "Some practice ancient Celtic rituals combined with popish religious ceremonies to rid their houses of restless spirits that they imagine take on animal shapes and rove about haunting the countryside. These dear folks live in fear, without the light of the Gospel of grace. They need our compassion, not our scorn. Motivated by just such compassion, ye ken John Nisbet who farms near the glebe in Newmilns?"

"Aye," said Angus.

"Years ago Nisbet's grandfather translated Holy Scripture into Old Scots so they could learn the Gospel of grace in their own language."

"Aye, Father," said Angus. "But did ye say Highlanders believe in evil spirits taking on animal form?"

"Aye, something like. They might see a hawk pass more than once overhead and claim it looks like a recently hanged prisoner, hanged for a crime he didnae commit, and come back to haunt them all for it."

"Would a Highlander think that of a crow?" asked Angus.

"Aye, and one that can talk," laughed Jennie.

"I'd be thinking many Highlanders would tremble in their kilt if they heard Flinch carrying on so."

"Father," said Jennie, "would ye be telling us again the story of the Irvine hangman? He was a Highlander, wasn't he?"

"Aye, a Highlander, indeed. Strathnaver Highlander named William Sutherland, he was. Brought up superstitious and illiterate, but eager for book learning, and wearied of the life of the Highlands, he moved to Ayrshire, where he swept chimneys and from time to time did the grim work of hangman for accused witches."

"Real witches?" said Jennie.

"Some of them were, alas, real witches, but we Lowlanders have our superstitions too, and many may have just been old or a bit odd in the head.

"As I was saying, William Sutherland was hangman in Ayr when we Covenanters rallied at the Pentland Rising and were defeated at Rullion Green in 1666."

A faraway gaze shone in Sandy M'Kethe's deep blue eyes, and he paused for several moments, as if seeing again those terrible days, his own imprisonment and impending hanging at Edinburgh, his son Duncan's gallant rescue, aided by Lindsay and his Royalist brother Hamish.

"Precious souls I fought withal," he continued, "John Short, the good butcher from Dalry, Alexander MacCulloch of Carsphairn, Cornelius Anderson, tailor from nearby Ayr, and nine others captured and sentenced by that unjust persecutor Lauderdale—all sentenced to death by hanging, as I was. But while these good and faithful men awaited the noose, illiterate Sutherland came often to see them in hopes of learning to read. Learned Covenanters that they were, they turned their cell into a school and over the weeks taught their would-be executioner to read."

"What book did they teach him to read?" asked Jennie.

"The Bible," replied their father. "Aye, they taught that once-barbaric Highlander to read Holy Scripture. And God's gracious Spirit by the Word began working faith in the man's heart. He was saved gloriously by the witness of those he was slated to execute on the gallows.

"As the day approached when Sutherland would be required to hang his new brethren, at first he resolved to run away. But while hearing a sermon text read, 'Ye have not yet resisted unto blood, striving against sin,' he longed to do more for the condemned men, and he determined to stand by their side.

"When the fateful order to hang the Covenanters finally came, Sutherland, the Highlander now turned Covenanter, flatly refused. The angry Provost seized him and threw him in the Tollbooth prison at Ayr, where they grilled him. All argument proved futile as Sutherland countered the urgings of the court with Bible texts. He refused to hang the men. Twin brutes, Dalyell and Drummond threatened the new Christian with the crushing tortures of the boot. To which he boldly replied, 'Aye, ye'll have to do better than that,' says he. 'Add the spurs, and while ye're about it boil me in lead, throw me in a barrel of spikes, and if that doesnae finish me, shoot me, hang me, but I'll not do yer dirty work and butcher these honest men, my brothers.' "

Angus felt a thrill of the hangman's boldness tingle down his spine.

"W-what did they do to him?" asked Jennie.

"That's the wonder of it, lass. They released him. They actually liberated the man."

"What happened to the condemned men?" asked Angus.

"Ah, that's the tragic part. The court settled their dilemma by bribing one of the condemned Covenanters, Cornelius Anderson, to save his own neck—by hanging his friends."

"He didnae do it?" asked Jennie.

"Aye, I'm afraid he was all too happy to."

"But how could he?" asked Angus.

"There's ever been in Christ's Kirk tares among the wheat, wolves among the sheep. Cornelius was a wolf. He lives today an outcast, mistrusted by both king and Covenanter. I shudder to think of the horrors that await him on the Judgement Day."

"While William Sutherland risked his own neck," said Jennie, "and gains the crown."

"Aye, and never forget—he was a Highlander. And if God can somehow extend his Sovereign grace to the likes of me and to the likes of ye, he can extend his grace to anyone, dragoons, archbishops, kings—aye, even Highlanders."

Angus studied the smooth-packed earth of the floor. Then, with pleading eyes, he looked up at his father.

A flicker of candlelight sparkled in the deep blue of his father's eyes looking intently back at his son. "Never presume on grace, lad. Never. It was bought at too great a price for us to go presuming on it."

"I'll bear it in mind, Father," said Angus softly. "And I thank ye."

"So, Father," began Jennie, looking up at the rafters and choosing her words slowly. "It was William Sutherland's virtue to take the risks he did for his brethren."

"Aye," replied their father warily. "And just where, lass, are ye taking me?"

"His risk was far greater," she continued, now looking intently at her father, "than any Angus and I would take going to help the Whytes, then."

Their father made no reply. Was the risk less? If only he could go along and protect them. But a grown man with musket and claymore—he'd bring down their fury.

"I'll care for Jennie, Father," said Angus. "And I'll have my bow."

"Oh, please, Father," said Jennie. "The Whytes do need us so. Please let us go?"

14 THE BARGAIN

Most mornings when it didn't rain Willy Whyte crossed the Irvine at the bridge and lumbered along the Scots pines on the south bank of the river across from the village of Newmilns. He loved the sights and smells of the forest. Birds, squirrels, and even rabbits scurried in all directions before his path, alarmed by the noise of his heavy tread, by his loud humming that from time to time burst forth into lines from the Psalter, and by his chattering to no one in particular. Laughing with glee, Willy would break into a heavy stumbling run for several steps, and when the creatures fled out of sight, he would resume his lumbering and his humming.

This morning Willy had flopped down on a large rock, his legs extended over one side of the rock and his head and shoulders over the other. With his hands he traced the path of an army of ants, his voice rising and falling as he reasoned with and, sometimes, scolded them. He had even assigned names to their leaders. Digging in his pockets, he then sprinkled tiny bits of crumbled oatcake and lint, and watched in delight as his ants gathered the feast.

Meanwhile, Angus and Jennie picked their way carefully

through the pines only a hundred yards from where Willy ruled over his little ant kingdom. With prayers and careful instructions, their father finally had agreed to their going. And he had agreed that Angus could bring Flinch along, but only after Angus demonstrated how putting a leather hood over the crow's head kept it from making any sound.

Looming in Angus's mind, however, was the problem of how to keep Willy quiet when he arrived. If Willy bellowed his usual greeting with his excited carrying on, all the Highlanders in the valley would hear. He had to keep Jennie from the Highlanders, for his father had laid a solemn charge on him to protect his sister at all costs. Angus intended to do so.

"There he is," said Jennie softly.

Many would have viewed the sight of a full-grown man in his fifties, lying on his belly on a rock, talking to the ants as an occasion for mocking hilarity, but for Angus and his sister, the scene only endeared their friend to them all the more.

"Nae, nae, yer lairdship Ross," they heard Willy scolding. "Ye must share with others. And Bishop Fraser, tut, tut, ye've gone and stolen from the Ramseys again. I *am* ashamed of ye."

"Just as I'd hoped," whispered Angus. "He's come for his walk on our side of the river."

"Aye, and he's having a wee chat with the ants, sweet man," said Jennie.

"Let's us close the distance," said Angus, "as silently as we can. I have a plan."

Dry pine needles carpeting the forest floor muffled their steps as Angus and Jennie crept from tree to tree closer to their friend. When only a few yards separated them from Willy, Angus, now lying on his stomach in a cool patch of shamrock and bracken fern, hissed, "Willy, Willy."

"*King* Willy, to ye," said Willy, not looking up from his play with the ants.

"Och, then, *King* Willy," said Angus, slithering closer. Jennie peered out from behind a tree.

Willy looked up and spotted Angus crawling toward him on the forest floor, Flinch, hooded, riding on his back. Willy's eyes bulged in wonder, then his face broke into a wide grin. Before he could scramble to his feet and yell in his excitement, Angus put his finger to his lips.

"Willy," he hissed. "We're playing a game. Ye must keep silent."

Angus and Jennie scrambled to their friend's side.

"Angus, Jennie, I'm so happy to be seeing ye," said Willy, barely able to contain himself. "Oh, and to see Flinch—though I'm most sorry about his head."

"Never mind his head," said Angus, pulling the hood aside, then quickly covering the bird again before it broke into cawing—or worse.

"We, too, are happy to see ye, Willy," said Jennie.

The ants now forgotten, only with great effort did Willy keep his voice low.

"Angus, Jennie, ye must meet my new friends who've come for a wee visit," said Willy, his eyes wide and eager.

Angus looked at Jennie.

"Aye, and who might they be?" asked Angus, glancing down at the ants.

"Poor folks," said Willy, nodding, a frown of sympathy on his fleshy face. "They donnae have enough to eat. So Father and Mother, bless their hearts, are feeding them."

"Feeding them?" repeated Angus.

"Aye, Father says, he says—" Here Willy lifted his broad puzzled face heavenward and bit his lower lip as he attempted to remember just what it was that Father says. "Och, he says, 'if yer enemy—' I cannae see as how they're our enemy—'if yer enemy hungers, feed him.' That there's what Father says, he does. And hae we fed them! They're so poor and hungry it seems we cannae fill them up."

"So ye've been good to them, Willy," said Jennie.

"Aye."

"And hae they been good to ye?" asked Angus.

Willy blinked rapidly, and his lower lip quavered as he considered the answer to Angus's question.

"They do roar so, from time to time. But Father says, 'Be patient. They donnae hae the best o' manners.' So Mother has set about to try and teach them how to talk right. I cannae understand much of what they say. They laugh my way a good bit. Oh, Angus, Jennie, ye must come meet them, then."

Angus felt his breath coming in short hot blasts. No doubt they did laugh a good bit Willy's way—cruel, mocking laughter.

"Maybe some other time, Willy," said Angus.

"We've come to see how *ye're* doing," said Jennie. "And we've brought some fresh-baked goodies for ye and yer mother and father."

Willy's eyes grew wide and a grin spread across his face. "I am ever so hungry," he said, rubbing his tummy. Sidestepping closer to the basket and biting his lower lip, he leaned over and sniffed the air for a hint of what lay within.

"Ye see, we've had to do without for our guests," explained Willy, nodding and lowering his voice in a confidential tone. "But Mother doesnae want them to ken."

"Willy, when do the Highlan—that is, yer guests," said Angus. "When do they leave the cottage?"

Willy looked across the river.

"They go to work," he replied. "And they must work ever so hard."

"Why do ye say that?" asked Jennie.

"Oh, they come back in the evening all staggering from

weariness," explained Willy. "Some of them hae worked themselves sick. Then we feed them and give them our beds."

"Would they be gone now, Willy?" asked Angus.

"We can see just there," said Willy, pointing through the trees. "When they go off, we'll see and hear them."

"Do they ever come back early?" asked Angus.

"If it rains," said Willy. "Or some other times, but not usually."

They watched the Whyte cottage in silence for several minutes. No friendly smoke curled from the chimney. *Elderly folks like the Whytes need a warm fire, and the Highland mob has no doubt used up all their fuel*, Angus thought bitterly.

Then, like flies stretching and preening when transformed from larvae, Highlanders emerged from the cottage, some still wrapping their great kilts about their middles and over their shoulders. All of them carried muskets and claymores, and pistols stuck out of wide leather belts.

"That's him," whispered Angus. "That's the clan chief I saw on the prowl last Sabbath day."

"Can ye be sure?" asked Jennie.

"Aye," said Angus, then turning to Willy. "Willy, do they play any games?"

"Aye, the tall one with the blue bonnet and feathers," said Willy. "He plays with kings and queens, and bishops and knights—oft times alone. I donnae ken the game."

When the last Highlander disappeared down the narrow street, Angus, leading Jennie and Willy, waded across the river.

The cottage was in shambles, and the elderly couple had already begun the hopeless task of making order out of the mess, hopeless because the Highlanders would only turn it all to havoc again when they came back. Jennie made the couple sit down and set about tidying the cottage for them.

"I'd heat up some broth, Angus," she said, "but the fuel's been all used up."

"Ye want me to go gather fuel?" he said. "And leave ye here—alone?"

"I'm hardly alone, Angus. Besides, there's a chill in the air, and the old couple need warmth. The more wood ye can gather the better. I'll bring some order here while you run back to the forest. It's just across the river. Ye can see the cottage all the while. Be quick and no harm'll befall any of us."

Angus hesitated. There was a chill in the cottage, and the clouds did look like rain. Jennie was right: the Whytes would need the warmth. He lifted hooded Flinch onto a rafter in the cottage and spun on his heel. After splashing across the river, he frantically loaded his arms with branches and sticks. Breathing hard he plunged back across the river and threw down his load. It would only last a few hours. Curse those foul thieves for robbing an old couple of their fuel.

From inside the cottage he heard Jennie and Willy's mother and father talking.

"Forget not hospitality." Mrs. Whyte was speaking loudly as if it were Jennie who was nearly deaf and not herself. "So says the Holy Scripture."

"Aye, for some hae entertained angels unawares," added David Whyte.

"Angels?" Angus heard Jennie's incredulous reply.

"Aye, and unawares. This, lass, would be one of the unawares times."

"I ken what ye're thinking, Jennie, dear," said Mrs. Whyte. "Ye're thinking there's little fear of these ones being angels in the end."

"So I was," replied Jennie.

"Fallen angels, more like," said the old man. "Nevertheless, I for one plan to obey God's Law and let our gracious Redeemer sort out the details."

Shaking his head in wonder, Angus turned and raced back across the river for more firewood.

With each load he was forced farther into the forest to find good wood. He felt a rising urgency with every step that took him farther from the cottage. His fifth load would be his last.

Then, he heard them. A raucous yelling, made sharp and penetrating by the expanse of the river—and it came from near the cottage.

Angus dropped the wood with a clatter at his feet and strung his bow. Then bolting toward the voices, he halted at the edge of the forest. No one was in sight, but from the open door of the cottage, he heard animal-like yelling.

"Tha mi ag iarraidh—"

It sent a chill down his spine. Another Gaelic voice rose from inside the cottage.

"Tha mi ag iarraidh—"

They want something. Angus gritted his teeth. Then, realization, like icy fingers gripped his heart. He knew what they wanted.

"Tha mi ag iarraidh am boirenach ad!"

"Am boirenach ad!"

He had to stop them. At least two of the Highlanders had returned and were, by the sounds of it, fighting—fighting over a woman. He understood that much of their Gaelic from the leering tones. And it had to be—Jennie. He had to stop them. Their voices rose in a warlike scream.

"Tha mi ag iarraidh am boirenach ad!"

If there were only two, Angus knew he could run them through with an arrow each—if he could only get them out of the cottage. But he'd have to be careful. An arrow that missed its mark might strike Willy or his parents—or Jennie. Then again, maybe the two brutes would do his work for him and tear each other apart in their frenzy.

Then, drawn by the yelling, six other Highlanders crowded the door of the cottage. Angus glanced at the clouds. The threatening rain must have drawn them all back. What could he do against eight armed Highlanders?

Taking large unhurried strides, their clan chief now appeared from around the cottage. *Make that nine armed Highlanders*, Angus thought in despair.

"Ogilvy! Macnab!" the man in the blue bonnet and feathers yelled, then he barked an order in Gaelic. The men parted and let him pass into the now silent cottage.

Riveted on the commotion, the men all stood with their backs to Angus. Grimly, he drew nine arrows and thrust them into the soft earth beside him. Would it be murder to shoot them—and in the back? Could he pick them all off one by one before they turned on him? They weren't crows. And what would happen to the Whytes—to the whole village—if he did kill them all? The other Highlanders would descend like the plague, and the valley would flow with innocent blood.

He unstrung his bow. He knew what he had to do. Angus gathered up the arrows and hid them with his bow in the bracken. Then, shooting anguished prayers heavenward, he plunged across the river. So intent were the Highlanders on what was going on inside the cottage, Angus was upon them before they could even turn around.

"Pardon me, gentlemen," said Angus, trying to keep his voice steady as he walked up to the door. "I have business with yer clan chief," he said firmly.

Six pairs of eyes turned suspiciously on Angus. Two of the men growled something in Gaelic. They smelled of unwashed wool, of whiskey, and of sweat. Would they let him pass?

"I have important business," called Angus, louder, "with yer chief. Let me pass."

"Who has business with me!" boomed the chief, appearing in the low doorway.

"Angus M'Kethe does," said Angus, his voice bold, though tremors fluttered through his insides like banners trembling in the wind before a battle.

"Och, and just *who* is Angus M'Kethe?" sneered the clan chief, waggling his head.

"That ye will find out," said Angus, "if ye'll consent to—a game of chess."

"Chess?" repeated the clan chief, stepping out of the doorway and looking Angus up and down with steel-gray eyes.

Angus looked into the cottage. On a bed in the corner sat the old man, one arm around his wife and the other around bewildered tearful Willy. Jennie sat rigid in a chair at the table, her eyes wide and staring straight ahead. On either side of her stood a Highlander, one stroking her hair and finishing each stroke by curling a strand of it around his finger. For an instant Angus felt the overwhelming urge to throw himself at the man's throat. He felt the convulsing muscles and the man's collapsing windpipe in his grip, and wondered if it would be murder. Either way, all would be lost if he did it. He must be patient. Flinch perched in the rafters above all, seemingly undetected as yet by the Highlanders.

"Chess, did ye say?" said the chief. "I only play the best. And I cannae be thinking that a young tike like yerself is among the best, laddie."

"But ye cannae be kenning so," said Angus, pulling a

chair up next to Jennie at the table. Her face seemed deathly pale, and her eyes pleaded with him. "Ye'll never ken if ye donnae play."

"Have ye ever played before, laddie?" asked the chief, pulling up a chair opposite Angus.

"I've not lost for over two years," said Angus.

"Then ye must hae been playing before ye were walking," said the chief.

A few of his clan who understood more English than the others burst into laughter at his jest. The Gaelic speakers joined in on the cue.

"White or black?" asked Angus by way of answer.

"Gather my board and pieces," barked the chief. "I'll be black. What stakes?"

"If I win," said Angus casually, "I'd like this cottage."

The chief looked around him and snorted. "This mess?"

"And," said Angus, looking levelly at the chief, "and I'll take back my sister, here."

"Och, my men, Ogilvy and Macnab, they've taking a wee bit of a fancy to yer sister. Ye might hae to contend with them for her."

"I'll contend with their clan chief for her," said Angus. "And I'll trust to yer honor as a man to deliver her and this cottage and all it contains up to me."

"That is," said the chief, with a reproving lilt, "if ye win."

"Aye, if I win."

The Highlander studied Angus over the table for several minutes.

"I've made an oath to my father . . . to bring back my sister," said Angus, "and her virtue."

"And ye think ye can do so," said the chief, "by beating me at chess."

"If ye'll play," said Angus. "And if ye're a man of yer word."

15 TREACHERY FOILED

Angus rested his chin on his clenched hands and studied the hand-whittled Highland chess pieces from eye level. Through the backs of his white ranks, he narrowed his eyes at the clan chief's knight. It looked more like a Highlander mounted on a pony than a real knight, but one thing was clear: the chief knew how to use every piece of his army. Angus scowled at the pawns. They looked ragtag, like rullion peasants, and the chief didn't hesitate to sacrifice them when it served his advantage. In fact, the only men Angus had taken were two pawns.

But Angus noted with satisfaction that within the first five moves of the chess game, the clan chief's condescending air vanished. He sat forward and studied Angus's face with a mixture of pleasure and kindled enthusiasm. Angus thought he detected even a hint of worry.

But if anyone was really worried, it was Angus. What would his father think of him playing chess for his sister's virtue? What if he lost? Could he keep his word and let the Highlanders have Jennie? Would it even be right to keep such a promise? He knew that if he lost he would have to come up with some other way to keep them from harming her. His father would never approve of hazarding his sister on a chess game. He studied the cold gray eyes of his opponent. The hair along Angus's neck rose and stood at attention. What would the clan chief do if Angus won?

With a nudge and a *thunk*, the chief swept in at an angle with his bishop and took one of Angus's pawns from the middle of the board. He too wanted to control the middle.

Angus drew in a deep breath to clear his head. He studied the board. He had to win. *Thank you, Mr. Clan Chief*, said Angus to himself. Clearing away the pawn opened the way for Angus to bring his queen into the fray, though, if he captured the popish-looking bishop, his queen would fall at the hands of the chief's knight. But he'd make his stand with his queen.

Slide, *Clunk!* The chief brought out his queen. *He's on the defensive*, mused Angus. He studied the chief's queen and thought he detected a resemblance to a picture he'd seen in one of the earl's books of Mary Queen of Scots, the enemy of John Knox and the Reformation. Clearly popish Highlanders carved these chess pieces.

Meanwhile, Ogilvy and Macnab grew restless and joined the other Highlanders loitering outside the cottage. They seemed to be engaged in some form of spitting contest, and amidst much hoopla, each man tried outdistancing the last spitter. The Whytes huddled in the corner, stroking and reassuring Willy, their words turning often to prayers of deliverance. Jennie slipped from the table when her persecutors left and joined the family in the corner. All the while, Flinch, his face hooded, perched silently above, and any scratching noise he did make blended with the rats rustling in the thatch.

An hour passed. And Angus's confidence grew. The chief was clever, but he was too rash with his moves at times. The results of that rashness lay in a growing pile of seized chessmen at Angus's side. Though the outcome was far from certain, Angus was hopeful.

As the game continued, the clan chief's face grew redder, and he frequently mumbled to himself in Gaelic. Angus thought he detected in the chief's manner a loss of enthusiasm for the contest.

Angus swallowed and ran his fingers through his hair. Sore losers don't keep their word. But he couldn't let him win. Maybe a draw would satisfy the man. Angus studied the board, and his mind systematically worked out the moves needed to end the game in a draw. Four moves. That's all it would take. But then whom would he keep? Jennie, of course. Then leave the Highlanders to plunder the Whytes? No. He had to win.

"I beg yer pardon, sir," said Angus, half an hour later. "But ye've put yer own self in check with that move."

"Aye, so I have. I just wanted to see if ye were paying attention, laddie."

Angus felt sweat trickle down his back. The clashing of steel came from outside the cottage. The chief's clansmen had left the spitting contest behind and now hooted and hollered as two of their number, grunting and swearing, honed their swordsmanship on each other. Heart-numbing fear gripped Angus's chest. There would be nothing to stop the clan chief from treachery if Angus won. He felt like a cornered hare. How did he get in this predicament? If only the clan chief would keep his word.

Angus scanned the few remaining chess pieces. His queen, knight, bishop, and his castle surrounded the chief's black queen and a stray pawn; he would have the chief in checkmate in two moves. If only the man would keep his word. *But, then*, thought Angus uncomfortably, *I have no intention of keeping my word if I lose. I'll do anything to protect Jennie. So what's the difference? Maybe there isn't any difference.*

The outcome of the game now secure in his mind, Angus sat back. He had to work this out. Maybe he should never have entered into the bargain in the first place: a young woman's life—his sister's life—gambled away on a chess game. But what else could he have done?

Then, words and phrases from his father's big Bible slowly began arranging themselves in his troubled mind. The chess game faded in his mind, and with an anxious imagination, he cried out in prayer, *Oh, Christ, my King . . .*

Protect me from my enemies;
Hide me from their conspiracies!
O, be our Refuge; come, draw near!
And trap our foe in his own snare.

Thud, thud, thud, went the chief's king as, with dark looks, he raised it by the crown and then keeping it upright with his fingers let it fall back onto the table with a thud. He did not lay it on its side, the symbol of defeat.

"Uh, check-checkmate, I believe it is . . . sir," said Angus.

The cottage grew ominously silent. No one dared to breathe. Only a slight rustling sound overhead could be heard along with the thudding of the chief's king.

"Aye, do ye think so, then?"

Thud, thud.

"Aye."

"But ye've gone and tricked me," said the chief, nodding as if working at convincing himself.

Thud, thud, thud.

"I have?"

"Aye, ye have. How was I to ken a tike—Lowland, Covenanter tike—could play a bit of chess? I didnae play my best for yer being a tike. That's how ye tricked me."

"But ye'll keep yer word," said Angus, "as ye are a man?"

Thud, thud, thud.

The clan chief turned and looked at the Whytes. Then he studied Jennie wordlessly. His gaze lingered on her longer than Angus liked. Their voices caught the attention of the chief's clansmen, who crowded into the cottage, led by the man called Ogilvy. The suffocating stench of unwashed men choked in Angus's throat, and his eyes began watering. They were trapped. There was no escape.

Then nodding at Jennie, as if to remind his chief what this was all about, Ogilvy said, "Tha mi ag iarraidh am boirenach ad."

He grinned. Broken and missing teeth left grotesque gaps in his mouth.

"But ye will keep yer word?" said Angus to the clan chief.

"Aye, it's my word," said the chief. "And I'll be keeping of it on my terms, laddie, not on yern."

"Then I'll just be taking my sister and be going," said Angus, rising to his feet.

On a signal from the chief, two pairs of hands fell on Angus's shoulders and pressed him back onto his seat.

"My word is," said the clan chief. "Ye can have the cottage and all it contains. I'll keep the woman. That's my word, and I'm keeping it."

Jennie tried unsuccessfully to suppress an involuntary sob. Angus ground his teeth together and clenched his fists. He couldn't bear to hear his sister's terror. But what could he do now? Oh, if only he'd killed them all and fled safely with Jennie. But now there was nothing he could do. He couldn't bring himself to look at Jennie. *Draw near, O God,* he prayed.

A scratching sound in the rafters caught his attention. As Ogilvy argued with his clan chief, Angus stole a quick glance up at Flinch. Perhaps prompted by curiosity at the sound of strange voices and the presence of men pressed in close below, or more likely due to the association with chocolate that went along with chess, Flinch had been clawing away at his leather hood so he could see. He'd just about succeeded.

Then, all that his father and William Cleland had told him of the superstitions of the Highlanders flooded his memory, and a desperate idea began to form in his mind.

He gave a soft whistle. With a flurry of black wings and a screech, Flinch descended out of the darkness of the rafters and landed on Angus's shoulder.

Startled, the clan chief narrowed his eyes at Angus. "What's this!"

Angus needed to get the most from Flinch. If ever he needed the bird to speak on command it was now. Ogilvy and the other Highlanders seemed to have forgotten Jennie for the moment. They looked warily at the bird that had just flown out of the rafters and landed on Angus's shoulder.

"I came upon him one day in a tree," said Angus, stroking the bird's shiny feathers. "He's not like other birds," continued Angus, lowering his voice.

"How not like?" demanded the chief.

"Look in his eyes," said Angus mysteriously. "I cannae exactly explain, but he's just not—like other birds."

Eyes wide, Ogilvy took a step closer to the bird and leaned over, looking intently at Flinch's oily black eyes. Flinch tilted his head to one side and cawed loudly in the man's face. Ogilvy nearly fell backwards in his fright. The other Highlanders laughed nervously.

"But there is something else about him," said Angus.

"There is?" said the chief.

"Without taking a stand on either side, mind ye, he'll tell ye where the loyalties lie in Scotland."

"He'll *tell* us!" said the chief, looking soberly at Angus. "Ye mean to say . . . this bird speaks?"

"Oh, he speaks, all right," said Angus.

"Demon if it did," mumbled one man.

Angus sent a silent prayer heavenward, while concealing a kernel of corn in his hand and passing it near Flinch's beak. He knew Jennie would be praying, too.

"Flinch, keen, clever Flinch, tell these gentlemen what they need to hear."

Angus held his breath. All eyes gazed at the bird. Flinch seemed to be enjoying the attention and looked deliberately from face to face.

Then, from his perch on Angus's shoulder, he beat the air with his wings and broke the tense stillness of the cottage with:

"King and Kirk! King and Kirk!"

Angus had not heard Flinch say the words more clearly.

"King and Kirk! King and Kirk!" continued Flinch.

"I-it speaks!" stammered Ogilvy, his eyes wide and roving.

"King and Kirk! King and Kirk!"

The clan chief sprang to his feet, his chair clattering to the floor behind him.

"Bheir leat a h-uile," he barked in Gaelic, "cal aca!"

The Highlanders quickly grabbed up the few remaining household items of any value in the cottage. Angus moved out of their way and joined Jennie and the Whytes in the corner. Jennie clung to her brother and would not let go for several minutes. With so little to take and the men eager to be gone, some just grabbed their weapons and left.

The clan chief hesitated at the door. He turned and his hand opened and closed on the hilt of his claymore as he fixed his gaze on Angus and the bird. For one heart-stopping moment Angus feared the man might draw his blade.

"We go," he said.

16 THE SHEARING

"So when Flinch started speaking," said Angus, nudging an ewe forward on the hindquarters, "the Highlander clan chief's eyes grew bigger and bigger, until they grew so big I was most afraid they'd go and pop out of his head."

"Clean out o' his head?" exclaimed Malcolm in wonder.

"Angus," said his father, his shearing clippers poised over a prostrate sheep. "Let's us have a wee bit less of yer swelling out of the story. Stick with what actually happened."

"And then what did happen?" asked Malcolm, his eyes wide and eager.

"The clan chief barked something in Gaelic, something about ordering his thugs to take with them everything that belonged to the Whytes. And they left."

"Tell it again! Tell it again!" squealed Malcolm.

"Tell it again, later," said his father. "Ye're not called to the free and easy life of a bard, Angus. Ye've other duties. Lend a hand, now. We hae sheep to shear."

"Aye, Father," said Angus, scooping up the warm mound of freshly sheared wool in his arms. He breathed in the sturdy smell of lanolin and felt the oily softness on his hands. His father helped right the naked-looking sheep, and then it scurried off in an embarrassed trot.

"Ye, Malcolm," said Angus's father. "Play dog. I need the next ewe—that one just there."

Malcolm, eager to help, bolted off in a wide arc around the ewe and feigned barking as he dodged in a zigzagging pattern until the sheep was in his grandfather's grip.

Angus's mother and sisters chatted nearby in the heather where they worked at sorting and cleaning the wool. Around the hearth, through the long northern winter, the women of the family would spin the wool into yarn and from the yarn knit warm socks, shawls, and bonnets. Throughout the year, they would sell or trade the wool goods to support the family.

Meanwhile, due to the increased worry over reparations for Sharp's murder, Angus's father had sent Duncan and Jamie to patrol the moor for any signs of impending danger and to gather what information they could. Angus set the fleece down in front of Jennie. After the events at the Whytes's cottage, Angus's determination to protect his sister grew even more intense. He would stop short of nothing to keep her safe—to keep his whole family safe. If only he could whisk them all away to some safe place. But there was another thing that troubled him.

"Father," he said, watching as his father expertly clipped away the wool as if he were merely helping the sheep off with its coat. "Should I hae done it?"

"Done what, lad?"

"Played chess for my sister," blurted Angus.

"Aye, gaming for a human life—the incongruity of it settles now into yer mind, lad."

"Aye. But I did want to shoot them all with my bow. I had nine arrows ready. They had Jennie—and the Whytes. I almost wish I'd killed them all."

"Wickedness gets complicated," said his father. "And the very wickedness we hate in others can creep over and clutch us in its foul grip. Though I cannae approve of gaming for yer sister, I am most glad ye chose a peaceful path over killing them."

"But would it hae been wrong to kill them? They were set to do so much harm."

"When ye're faced with that crossing, it always comes down to loving yer neighbor as yerself. And loving yer neighbor—in this case including yer dear sister—might mean protecting them from an evildoer. And protecting them from an evildoer might mean using force against the evildoer. And that force might lead to the unhappy, unwelcome necessity of killing the evildoer. Mind ye, followers of King Jesus love life and must always be the most reluctant to raise their weapons against anyone. God takes no pleasure in the death of the wicked—and nor ought we."

"Aye, Father. But what about my word to the clan chief? I agreed that if I lost the chess game, I'd give up Jennie and the Whytes."

"Would ye hae kept yer word, lad?" asked his father, pausing and eyeing his son levelly.

"That's just it. When I did win, the clan chief didnae keep his word, and if it hadnae been for Flinch, I cannae bear to think of what they would hae done to Jennie."

"If ye'd lost, lad?"

"I'd hae never been able to look my sister in the face," said Angus with feeling, "if I'd not broken my word and done all I could to protect her. But is that right, Father. Before God? Is it right?"

His father straightened to his full height and eyed his son, the sheep at his feet only half sheared.

"The clan chief broke his word to do evil. Ye would have

broken yers to do good to yer sister. And in doing so, ye would've restrained the evil of those wicked men. To have kept yer foolish oath would have been to heap a greater sin upon the folly of yer oath."

"But, Father, what of the psalm that tells us the man who walks in the Lord's presence 'keeps his oath even when it hurts.' What of that?"

"When it hurts *himself*, lad. He keeps his oath even when it costs himself a great deal. But ye keeping yer oath would hae cost *others* a great deal. Ye had a higher obligation to protect yer loved ones. No perceived obligation to an oath must ever turn ye aside from that higher obligation."

"So would it hae been a sin to break my word, then?

"We're to let our yea be yea, and our nay, nay, lad. Don't ye go imagining that because this came right in the end, that taking a foolish oath is a good plan for the future. Put yer hope in God and take only oaths that reflect that hope—and keep yer word."

"But was it a sin?"

"I donnae ken. But I do ken that sinning is of many degrees. To hae left Jennie in their hands would hae been a far greater sinning. Mind ye, God is not responsible for putting us in circumstances where we're compelled to choose one sin over another, but sometimes it seems we in our folly put ourselves in just such dilemmas. Though things came out all right in the end, playing chess for yer sister, lad, ought not to be thought of as a good strategy in the future."

"I ken that now, Father. But what will happen next?"

His father's eyes fell on the women and children laughing and working nearby. He frowned.

"I fear, lad," he said, his voice low, "that reprisals for Sharp's murder will rain upon us any day now. Even now Claverhouse is sharpening his sword and enlisting and arming more dragoons for the killing that will surely come. I fear it, lad. And we must be on the constant alert for it all."

"Could we flee?"

"Flee? Where would we go, lad? I've already fled from Inverary and from Dalry. Where to from here?"

"Many hae gone to Holland. Richard Cameron studies there in exile, and the earl has been and may be forced to go there again soon."

"But it costs money to live in Holland. We have many mouths to feed. And we have no money for passage to Holland. Ye hae no idea, Angus, how much money it would cost to live in Holland."

"The earl says that some Covenanters are making plans to flee to the Carolinas in the New World."

"The Carolinas?"

"Aye, English Puritans have gone and established prosperous colonies in a place called America, where land is rich and plentiful, great forests abound, and the fishing is good. They live in peace and safety free from bishops and far from the clutches of King Charles. What's more, they worship God freely. Oh, Father, may we go?"

His father ran his fingers through his beard in thought.

"We have no money. Sell all our few sheep and anything we have of value and we might have enough passage for one of the family. But while I live I'll not flee and leave a single bairn behind. No, it cannae be."

Angus knew his father was right, but he longed for safety—and for freedom.

"There is another thing, Angus," said his father. "I love Scotland. I couldnae bear to leave my beloved Scotland behind never more to see the heather spreading away across the moors, never to see her wee shady glens and her bonny braes. No, Angus, I couldnae bear it."

With that, his father bent and resumed shearing the patient sheep. Angus gathered up the fleece and laid it out for cleaning by the womenfolk, but he couldn't stop thinking about the New World and about freedom.

"But, Father," said Angus several minutes later. "If there was a way, ye'd leave Scotland for freedom, wouldn't ye, freedom to worship?"

"The Lord kens how much I long to worship him, how much I long for my bairns to worship him. But fleeing means giving up on Scotland, on Scotland's freedom to worship God. I cannae do that. By remaining we may do some good. By fleeing we leave our beloved Scotland to the devil. I cannae do that."

17 RENDEZVOUS OF REBELLION

When the last clean white and naked-looking sheep newly shorn of its winter wool grazed nearby, and the final fleece was gathered up, Angus's father proposed another fencing lesson with the claymore. Malcolm jumped up and down gleefully on the sidelines.

"Ye've got 'im now, bravo, Grandfather!" shouted Malcolm.

Angus found himself feeling a bit resentful at his nephew's cheering, and determined to do better, he made a lunge at his father.

Sandy M'Kethe neatly parried the thrust, disengaged, and made a returning lunge, the sword point stopping just short of Angus's neck. Chin in air, Angus looked down the blade at the deep blue of his father's eyes and tried to swallow. What would it be like to gaze, for one final instant, down the much-used blade of a monster like Claverhouse? He shuddered.

"We'll halt just there, then," said his father, stepping back and saluting with his claymore. "Ye're making some progress, lad. Donnae be discouraged. I've been at the sword a wee bit longer than ye."

Expelling his breath and wiping his brow, Angus tossed

the claymore aside and collapsed onto the sod. If only he could just stick with the bow.

"What's this?" said his father, looking steadily down the moor. "Aye, it's the lads."

Angus saw the dark curly hair of his brother-in-law, Jamie, and the red tangle of Duncan's head just appearing at the break in the moor. They seemed to be running or at least loping along as if eager to return, and they carried their muskets at the ready.

"Angus, let's us go meet them," said his father, casting a quick glance at where the women and children worked. "No sense in the latest tale of woe upsetting the women and the wee ones."

When Duncan and Jamie saw them coming, they halted, and Duncan waved a piece of paper wildly in the air. Angus and his father quickly joined them.

"Lads, ye look like ye've seen a ghost," said their father.

Neither of the young men spoke.

"What have ye in yer hand, Duncan?" asked his father.

"He's done it now," said Duncan, shaking the paper in his fist.

"Who's done what?" asked his father.

"King Charles has," said Duncan, slapping the back of his hand on the paper. "And it's all right here."

Their father took the paper and began to read.

" 'Charles, by the grace of God, king of Great Britain, France and Ireland, defender of the faith—' "

" 'Defender of the faith'?" cried Duncan, his voice quavering with emotion. "Can ye believe the reach of this tyrant?"

"Let me read it out, Duncan," said his father. " 'Forasmuch as, albeit by the fundamental laws of all monarchies, the power of arms is lodged in the king, and the rising in arms . . . under false pretext of religion and conscience . . . or upon any pretext whatsoever, to rise or continue in arms, it should be high treason to the subjects of this kingdom.'

"The man robs us of our last civil defense," said their father, his brow furrowing.

"Go on, Father," urged Duncan. "It grows worse still."

" 'If any person should take up arms against us,' " he continued reading, " 'they are declared traitors and should suffer forfeiture of life, honor, lands, and goods, as in cases of high treason.' "

"Aye, and now he crushes our field worship like squashing a midge," said Duncan bitterly, bringing his fist down in his palm with a slap. "He calls our meetings 'rendezvous of rebellion.' He declares just here, that 'such as frequent those meetings, do go there in arms upon a criminal and treacherous design.' And he orders his officers—that'd be his favorites, like Claverhouse—to rigorously proceed against us as traitors. And look down here, Father. The king requires all his judges and officers to put his 'commands in vigorous execution, even against those who frequent those meetings *without arms*.' Can ye be believing that? Unarmed women and bairns are now guilty of high treason for bearing arms—even when they're *not* bearing arms!"

"And their lives are forfeited for it," said Jamie soberly. "This is surely the work of Sharp's original bill against arms."

"No doubt," agreed their father.

"Sounds like this proclamation is high treason," said Angus.

"Aye," said their father. "Dated, 13 May, 1679, that'd be nearly a fortnight ago. Did ye discern if it's been acted upon?"

"Most cruelly, Father," said Duncan, his voice shaking. "Though Claverhouse and the king's officers have been acting on this proclamation long before now, it grows worse. The Dingwalls ferm-toun on the verge of the moor was set upon by a troop of horse."

Duncan broke off and gazed into the distance.

"And?" said their father.

"They'd shot or hacked all their flock to death," continued Duncan. "The poor slaughtered creatures littered the moor round about the cottage."

"The soldiers had dumped out what remained of their oats and corn," added Jamie. "And then trampled all in the dung."

"And the cottage?" asked their father.

"Burned," said Duncan, "and walls pulled down."

Angus pictured the dreadful scene in his mind: the musket firing, the reeking smoke, the bleating of lambs, the brutal shouts of soldiers about their bloody work.

"And the Dingwalls?" Their father asked the question.

Angus dreaded to hear the answer.

Duncan and Jamie stared meaningfully back at their father.

"We buried five bodies," said Jamie at last, his voice husky and strained. "Two were bairns. The biggest had no more than eight years—Malcolm's age."

Angus could not quite imagine the horror of those last minutes for the children. Did their parents fall first in full view of the terrified little ones? Or were the parents forced to watch as the children were put to the sword?

"The bloody work of Claverhouse," said Duncan. "It's his way: killing women and bairns."

"Poor William," said their father, his face strained with anguish. "Poor William Dingwall, his wife and wee ones cut down with none to rescue them."

"But I think William was away," said Jamie. "The three grown-ups—they were women."

"Or they dragged him off," said Duncan. "To save him for the cruelties of the screws or the gallows."

"Either way, he'll be desperate to avenge them," said their father.

"And all this done in obedience to the king's command," said Angus.

"It behooves us to make ready at all times for Claverhouse," continued their father. "Duncan, Jamie and I will take turns guarding and watching our ferm-toun. Angus, ye'll help, too. And we must do what we can to help protect our neighbors from the Dingwall's fate."

"Och, Claverhouse can pillage and murder in the king's name," said Angus. "But when we take up arms to defend women and bairns, we're guilty of high treason. Father, will justice ever reign in Scotland?"

"In God's time, it will, lad," said his father.

"Surely not while Charles lives," said Duncan.

"How *do* we honor such a king?" asked Angus.

"I donnae ken, lads," said their father. "But we must fear God and do our best to honor the king. How, in times like these, I donnae pretend to ken. But we begin by praying for him, praying that he lives up to his name, Defender of the faith."

"But *pray* for him, Father?" said Duncan. "I ken I shouldnae say it. But I'd rather see him burn in hell."

18 BIRTHDAY BONFIRES

"Morag stopped in for a wee visit," said Mary M'Kethe to her husband, next evening.

"Aye," he said.

"Morag says, 'Tomorrow's the king's birthday,' says she." Mary M'Kethe ladled broth into wooden bowls for supper as she spoke.

Angus swallowed, and his stomach rumbled as he sniffed the steaming aroma of the mutton and barley soup.

"Ah so," said her husband.

"Aye, but she didnae stop there. Says Morag, 'The king's gone and proclaimed a holiday to celebrate his birthday, and,' says she, 'to celebrate his restoration to the throne.' "

"Aye, but what kind of a man imposes a holy anniversary day to be observed throughout the realm—and all for himself?" asked Jennie. She brought the bread knife down with a smack and sawed off another slice from the still-steaming loaf.

"Holy?" said Angus incredulously.

"Aye, set aside for rejoicing and thanksgiving at his birthday," said their mother, "and for his restoration to the throne in 1660. I for one, as is Morag, am having a wee bit of a difficult time stirring up much rejoicing and thanksgiving over the occasion."

"As are we all," admitted Sandy M'Kethe. "But we may take some comfort in the fact that he has chosen to be our enemy, not we his. O, how I do long for the day when peace and justice are restored to our benighted land."

"But can it ever be," asked Jennie, "while such a one as Charles sits on the throne?"

"Our Redeemer, lass, is in the business of changing king's hearts. And thus, we continue to fix our hope in God and pray that he gives us patience and perseverance in our trials."

Angus brought his foot down on a spider scurrying across the hard-packed earth floor—and twisted his toe. He wasn't any too sure about the likelihood of Charles having a change of heart, at least not before the Judgment Day.

"The earl told me about the king's new paintings commissioned for his palace in Edinburgh," said Angus after the family had sat down around the trestle table and his father had offered thanksgiving for their food.

"At Holyrood Palace?" said his mother. "Hard by the old abbey? I didnae ken Charles ever came to Holyrood."

"I think he's only been once," said Jennie. "So I've heard. Prefers London society and his palace at Winchester to Scotland."

"Nevertheless, he's spent heaps renovating the place," said Sandy M'Kethe. "Costly tapestries from Italy, magnificent terracotta ceilings—and the paintings."

"I suppose he has to spend all the cess tax on something," said Mary M'Kethe bitterly, "and his take from the plunderings."

"What are the paintings of?" asked Jennie.

"They're supposed to be of Scottish monarchs," replied Angus, dipping a hunk of bread in the rich broth. "Big as life, floor to ceiling, stretching away down both sides of the great hall, from ancient times up to himself. But the earl says the ancient ones are all faked—King Ferguson somebody and the lot, all made-up kings. Never even breathed." He tore off a bite of bread and chewed slowly.

"Why would he do that?" asked Jennie.

"Make up for his father being beheaded, I should think," said Sandy M'Kethe. "During Cromwell's time, monarchs had a pretty bad name. Charles is setting about to fix all that by showing a long continuous line of royalty all leading up to—himself."

"So he's even trying to rewrite history, then," said Angus.

"So it would seem," replied his father. "I'm inclined to think that tyrants always set about shaping history after their liking."

"Has the earl seen the paintings?" asked Jennie.

"Aye," said Angus. "Charles wants all his nobles to see them."

"Are they beautiful paintings?" asked Jennie a little wistfully.

"Maybe. But the earl says there is something very peculiar about them," replied Angus.

"What is it?"

"Charles ordered the painter—man from Holland—to paint Charles's own face on each one of them. So as ye walk down the long hallway, says the earl, staring down at ye is the face of Charles in every painting. From the faked ones right up to his tyrant self."

"Even Mary Queen of Scots' face looks like Charles'?" asked their mother.

"So says the earl."

"Och, this king's a more vain, pompous fool than ever I thought," said Mary M'Kethe. "How much did all this cost?"

"Thousands, I'm sure," said her husband. "And may the Lord guard us from such vanities."

"Little fear of that," said his wife, looking side to side at the rough and humble walls. "But I ken we're more blessed without the frills. Rid me of this dissembling, Covenant-breaking king and all his tyranny, and I'd be content indeed."

"Aye, Mary, m'love," said her husband. "But our lot is to fear God and find our contentment in his providence, even with such a king and all our woes. And why? Because he has promised us that each woe is for our sanctification, he has. Aye, and so we rest in God."

"But we're to honor the king, too," said Jennie, bewildered furrows on her brow.

"Aye, that we are," said their father, running his fingers through his beard and gazing into the hissing peat fire.

"But how?" asked Angus. "Do we light the bonfire and celebrate his restoration and birthday as the king commands? Do we show him honor by celebrating the day that began all our woe? Or do we make a stand against his evil deeds?"

"Aye," added Jennie. "What would Mr. Welsh say?"

"There are few more worthy than he," said their father. "And I honor him for urging us to seek peace both with the king and with one another. His role is first preaching, not fighting. I ken that neither Mr. King nor Mr. Welsh would sanction open rebellion against the king. Och, the Lord kens I have labored much in prayer over what it is we are to do," continued their father. "Aye, and peace-loving man that I am, I'm nevertheless inclined to think that there are times when fearing God means standing against the injustice of the king. Not in active rebellion, mind ye, but nor by celebration and giving public show of support for his evil schemes. As I am a Christian, we'll light no bonfire."

"What will the others do?" asked Angus.

"I believe some will make a greater show of standing against Charles's wickedness than merely not lighting bonfires and celebrating."

"Will some rise up and fight him?" asked Angus. He felt his heart pounding faster in his chest, but grope about in his mind as he did, he couldn't tell for sure why, "—a-and we with them?"

"I want peace, lad. God above kens I want it. But it might come to fighting in the end, fighting to protect yer mother and Jennie, Fiona and Lindsay, and the wee bairns from their cruel grasp. Aye, it might come to fighting for justice so as to win that peace. I donnae ken. I only hope there's some other way."

19 RUTHERGLEN BURNING

Thursday, May 29, 1679, dawned clear and fair. Nevertheless, as Angus led his flock up the moor to pasture for the day, he felt a sort of skittering uneasiness in his mind, like when sheep sense thunder in the wind. The freshly sheared flock looked lily white against the green and purple of the moor grass and heather, and they looked scrawny and vulnerable without their fleecy wool coats.

As his father had buckled on his claymore and tucked a brace of loaded pistols in his belt that morning, he had urged Angus to take special care and keep his eyes alert for any danger. Duncan and Jamie would again act as an armed patrol to warn and protect other neighbors on the moor. On the king's holiday, the M'Kethe family's work would proceed as usual: no celebration, no bonfires, work as usual. And all in defiance of the king's command.

Keeping his uphill stride, Angus spun in a complete circle, eyes scanning every twist and weave of the moor for trouble. And it wasn't crows he looked for now. A shadow came over his mind as he thought what it must have been like for the Dingwall women—and the children—as bloody Claverhouse in his lace-trimmed armor and his leering dragoons descended like vultures on the helpless family. He shook his head, trying to clear the grim reconstruction from his mind. Gripping his bow, he mentally rehearsed the rapid motion that would turn it from a harmless walking stick into a deadly weapon. Even Flinch, preening on his shoulder, sensed the tension that hung ominously in the air.

Halting just below a ridge strewn with man-sized boulders, Angus turned the sheep out to crop the grass in a shallow glen. Scrambling to the encircling ridge, Angus strung his bow and jabbed three arrows in the sod at the ready. Facing his flock and the north, he sat back against a large granite stone patterned with orange lichen and flecked with quartz that glimmered in the sunlight like tiny eyes. He critically scanned the view. There lay the Irvine valley, Loudoun Hill, and away to the west, the village of Newmilns. Satisfied with his position, he then rose onto his knees and peered over the boulder to the barren south. If anyone approached for good or ill, he would see them coming and be ready.

After half an hour of alert watching, Angus had seen nothing out of the ordinary. He fingered the earl's book inside his bag and then drew it out and opened it. He could read and be on his guard at the same time.

> The Porter, Watchful, perceiving that Christian made a halt, cried unto him, "Is thy strength so small? Fear not the lions, for they are chained, and are placed there for trial of faith. Keep in the midst of the path and no hurt shall come unto thee."

Flinch flew from Angus's shoulder onto the open book and pecked at the pages.

"Leave off, then, Flinch," said Angus, flicking the bird's beak with his finger and resuming his reading.

> Then I saw that he went on, trembling for fear of the lions, but taking good heed to the directions of the Porter; he heard them roar, but they did him no harm.

Angus frowned. If this was an allegory, as the earl said, then this meant something more. They had lions aplenty hieing at their heels and roaring, but he hadn't noticed any chains. What's more, these lions do more than roar; they devour, too. *Maybe this Englishman didn't get things right in this book after all*, mused Angus. *Unless*, he wondered, *maybe there were chains on even these lions, chains that he could not see*.

"King and Kirk! King and Kirk!" called Flinch, walking sideways along the book and bowing as he called.

Angus looked from the page to the bird and back to the page. Throughout the day Angus alternately read and watched, read and watched. He was particularly moved by the injustice of the trial and the condemnation of one called Faithful.

> They therefore brought him out, to do with him according to their law. First they scourged him, then they buffeted him, then they lanced his flesh with knives, after that they stoned him with stones, then pricked him with their swords, and last of all they burned him to ashes at the stake. Thus came Faithful to his end.

It seemed so real that Angus imagined he smelled the smoke of that burning. With a stitch of his breath, he realized that it had been several pages since he'd checked for trouble. He rose quickly to his knees and studied the countryside. Then he looked north. Smoke rose from three or four places in the valley. Not the narrow curling peat smoke that ordinarily rose from the cooking fires in the cottages. Large columns of black and gray smoke rose and sparks flew upward from the source.

Rutherglen

Claverhouse at his bloody work? Angus wondered. Or were these the king's bonfires, lit to celebrate his birthday and restoration? No doubt the drunken vicar at Loudoun Parish Kirk saw to the lighting of at least one of the fires, and there were other Royalists. It made Angus sick. With a whistle he gathered his flock and strode down the moor for home, casting dark looks at the ascending columns of smoke as he went.

***

". . . Ruthless and impetuous people, who sweep across the whole earth to seize dwelling places not their own," read Angus's father that evening after supper. Knitting needles clicked rhythmically in the background, and tallow candles hissed and sputtered as they cast their shadowy light on the faces, young and old, of the gathered clan.

His voice rose and fell with the words of the ancient prophet. "They are a feared and dreaded people; they are a law to themselves and promote their own honor. Their horses are swifter than leopards, fiercer than wolves in the night. Their cavalry gallops headlong; their horsemen come from afar. They fly like vultures swooping to devour; they all come bent on violence. Their hordes advance like a desert wind and gather prisoners like sand."

His father's strong voice ended, and Angus watched him slowly close the big book.

"This, too, is the word of the Lord," he said.

"Father, it sounds just like King Charles and bloody Claverhouse at their work," said Angus.

"Aye, Habakkuk was a prophet indeed," said Duncan.

"But we must take heart from this," said Sandy M'Kethe.

"Take *heart* from it?" said Jennie. "I admit, I feel a rising fear in my breast when I hear of it."

Angus glanced at his sister. Candlelight sparkled in her wide eyes as she looked intently at their father. There was fear in that look.

"We're not alone. The wicked have hemmed in the righteous before us," said Sandy M'Kethe. "Justice has many times before now in Scotland been perverted by wicked men. That knowledge should keep us from self-pity and despair. And it should make us long all the more for true justice."

His words were suddenly interrupted when a staccato of pounding sounded on the door.

Angus felt his pulse quicken, and he heard his mother sharply draw in her breath. Fiona gathered the twins in her arms and rocked them as much to comfort them as herself. In an instant Sandy M'Kethe leapt to his feet and reached for his claymore. Duncan and Jamie joined him, and Angus strung his bow and set an arrow on the string.

Another volley of loud knocking shook the door.

"Have no fear," a muffled voice called. "It's William Cleland, and I bring ye news."

Angus's father threw the door open and young William entered the croft. Sandy M'Kethe searched the blackness outside for any other signs of life before securing the door once again.

"What news?" demanded Angus's father.

"Ye no doubt saw the fires today in the valley?" began William.

"Aye, we did," said Angus. "Three or four set in Newmilns alone."

"Aye, and others were laid about the countryside," said William. "Most notably near Glasgow at Rutherglen, some few folks singing and making merry to the king about the conflagration. What's more, new ranks of the king's forces hae come from Lanark and are garrisoned nearby—"

Angus offered his friend a stool near the fire. William straddled it, and his eyes flashed as he warmed to the storytelling.

"—When up to the market cross gallops Sir Robert Hamilton and the minister Mr. Thomas Douglas, supported by eighty stout and able men, who, against the king's proclamation, came in arms."

"What men?" demanded Sandy M'Kethe. "Men faithful to the Covenant or no?"

"Faithful men, all. And all resolved to make public show of loyalty to Christ the Redeemer and to show their determination to resist Charles's wicked ways."

"How did they do it?" asked Angus eagerly.

"They judged it their duty to add their names to the worthies who've gone before and 'suffered imprisonment, fining, forfeitures, banishment, torture, and death from an evil and perfidious adversary to the Church and kingdom of our Lord Jesus Christ.' I worked at memorizing that bit there."

"What did they do next?" asked Angus.

"Aye, next they took up copies of all the acts and proclamations of the king against our Convenanted reformation, including those acts that ousted the faithful ministers from their pulpits, those acts forcing bishops on the Kirk, those acts against field meetings and preaching, and against the presumptuous act of imposing this holy anniversary day for the king."

"What did they do with them all?" asked Angus.

William grinned. "A great bonfire billowed at the market cross ready to hand. They cast all these acts and declarations of the king against the Covenant into the blaze, and did so just 'as the king's men have unjustly, perfidiously, and presumptuously burned our sacred Covenants.' I memorized that bit, too."

"Then what did they do?" asked Angus's father.

"When the flames had consumed all the king's proclamations," continued William, "Hamilton and Mr. Douglas stomped out the king's bonfires and affixed their testimony and declaration on the market cross. From there they retired to Newmilns, where I picked up the story of it all, as did the earl. Mr. Douglas is to preach at the field meeting on the Sabbath Day at Laird Hamilton's lands at Drumclog. Perhaps we shall all hear more said of the deed then."

"Perhaps we shall," said Sandy M'Kethe pensively. He ran over in his mind what he knew of the field meetings that would gather on the Sabbath. Mr. Welsh would be preaching north toward Stirling—too far to travel with womenfolk and the wee ones. And Mr. King would preach closer, near the village of Hamilton, but still too far.

"And, perhaps, we shall all meet bloody John Graham of Claverhouse there, too," said Mary M'Kethe. "Stirred up like a hornet."

"But he'll not be there to hear Gospel preaching," said Duncan. "Of that we can be most certain."

"I'm told the wife of Claverhouse," continued William, "says that if she ever was forced to hear Presbyterian preaching, she'd want the house to fall down upon her head."

"She doesnae ken, poor woman," said Mary M'Kethe, "that it's just that preaching that brings down on our miserable heads the saving mercy of God. Poor woman, indeed. But mark ye," she continued, "the king's horde are sure to see this as a rising."

"Do ye ken what Claverhouse will do in response?" asked Angus.

"Word is he's on the prowl near Fenwick and plunders again at Lochgoin farm," replied William. "He's moving south."

"Aye, he'll bend all to crush the rising," said Sandy M'Kethe. "But then, by God's might, we shall bend all to make ready for him."

20 SWORD IN THE HAY

Angus flattened himself down as low in the heather as he could. He looked to his left. His father hunkered beside him, eyes studying every detail of the heather-thatched croft and low stone barn that made up the Blantyre farm.

"All's quiet," hissed his father. "A bit too quiet, I fear."

It was Saturday morning, and his father had left Duncan and Jamie to guard their ferm-toun. With a gnawing uneasiness in his stomach and that uncomfortable pounding in his chest, Angus had obeyed his father's order to ready himself. Angus had gathered up his bow and arrows and had followed his father to do what they could for their neighbors. His father had ordered him to leave Flinch home with the pigeons.

"It doesnae look like anyone's home," whispered Angus.

"Aye, so it looks," said his father warily. He turned and carefully scanned the hills surrounding the farm.

"Where's all their stock?" asked Angus. "I see no sheep, and didnae the Blantyres keep a cow?"

"Aye, they did."

"I donnae see any cow."

They watched in silence for several minutes.

"I'm going inside," said his father. "Old Blantyre or his wife may be ill—or wounded. Angus, ye guard the door, and donnae take yer eyes off these hills. If ye see anything, call out and scatter like the wind."

Angus watched as his father drew near the low doorway. He hesitated at the door, turned, and made a slow sweep of the hills with his eyes. Then, pushing open the door, he lowered his head and disappeared inside the croft. Angus scrambled to his feet and ran to the open door.

From here he could see a wide panorama to the north—the most likely direction from which visitors might come. He studied the treeless pasture rising to barren moorlands that surrounded the farm, then he glanced nervously up at the glowering clouds. It looked as though even God was against them. He strained to hear, and even the croaking of a frog made him start in alarm as if it were the rasping bellowing of Claverhouse himself. Angus couldn't remember being anywhere that made him feel more unprotected.

He waited. What was his father finding inside? An involuntary shudder skidded down his neck and back. Try as he might, he couldn't get out of his mind what the dragoons did to the Dingwalls. Had the Blantyres' things been plundered, all their sheep, their cow carried away? Worse yet, had they been brutally murdered in their bed? But then, Claverhouse and his dragoons ordinarily left behind them devastation like a whirlwind, and they almost always burned everything standing.

"Nothing." His father's voice startled him from behind. "It looks as if they left in haste. But things donnae look plundered like."

"How long ago did they leave?" asked Angus. "And why?"

"There's hot coals in the grate."

Angus swallowed and scanned the hills. "Do ye think they got warning and fled?" He felt a creeping on the back of his neck.

"Might have. We check the barn, lad, and then we go. Watch at the door."

Angus heard his father rummaging in the hay inside the barn. "Anything, Father?"

"Just hay," came the muffled reply.

Suddenly, Angus felt and heard the muffled thudding of horse on the sod. Not just one horse. It sounded like five or six, but where were they?

"Father! Horses!"

"Where?" demanded his father, running to the door.

"I donnae see them to the north," said Angus.

"Too close," said his father, grabbing Angus by the belt and yanking him into the barn. "We cannae bolt for the heather. They'll see us for sure."

"Is . . . is it Claverhouse and his dragoons?" Angus's mouth was almost too dry to form the words.

"Like as not. We must hide and hide well," said his father, turning and taking stock of the barn. He gripped Angus by the shoulders. "Angus, ye make for the loft. Hide deep down in the hay. And may God deliver ye, my lad."

"Where will ye hide?" asked Angus, starting up the ladder.

His father drew his claymore and lifted up a pile of straw near the door. Clutching his dirk in his other hand, he rolled under the straw and lay still. "Here in the straw." He parted the straw with his dirk and looked lovingly at Angus. "God be with ye. Now go, lad. Hide—hide well."

Angus ran up the rungs of the ladder. He knew why his father had chosen a hiding place on the ground floor of the little barn so near the entrance. Dragoons would be more likely to discover him, and then he'd create some kind of diversion so Angus could escape. He knew that's why his father had done it, and he doubted that any soldier would get past his father even if they didn't discover him first. Angus wanted more than anything to get free of these dragoons. He remembered with a shudder the evil cruelty they had done to the Dingwalls, but he did not want the dragoons to find his father.

Angus dove deep into the hay and lay on his back. He heard his father below shuffling around in the straw, getting into position. With pounding heart, he heard the snorting and stamping of horses being reined in just outside the door. With a shout from the commander and amidst the rattling of leather harness and the clanking of swords, the soldiers dismounted.

"I want this dump of a farm razed to the ground," yelled the commander. "Seize anything of value. And use the only cure for the plague of Presbyterianism on the rest. Kill it."

It has to be Claverhouse, thought Angus, his mind screaming in protest at it all. Why such brutality and hatred? How many others like the Dingwalls had been hiding out for their life just as he was, only to be found and murdered by these monsters? Would they find his father? Would they find him?

"Ye four," barked Claverhouse, "search the house. Ye there, young Corporal Boig, ye're green at this business. Ye take the barn apart. Like vermin, these Presbyterians like hiding in straw. Use yer sword to find 'em."

Panic siezed Angus by the throat. He didn't want to die by the random thrust of some dragoon's sword while cowering in the hay. He'd rather face his enemy with weapons in hand.

The scraping of boots on the packed earth floor of the barn made Angus's blood run cold. He held his breath. The hay made him itch, but if he moved a muscle he knew he'd be discovered.

The sliding of the blade against the metal scabbard seemed to go on and on as the young officer drew his sword. Angus gasped for air, and he felt an almost uncontrollable urge to tear aside the hay and let fly with his arrows. If the man found his father, he would do just that.

Holding his breath, Angus heard the first thrust of the sword shying through the straw. It ended with a clunk against stone. O, *Lord, make him miss my father,* Angus prayed through clenched teeth.

Another thrust of the officer's sword in the hay, another clunk against stone.

What would his father be thinking as each thrust of the sword came closer? He'd be praying, Angus knew. *But is the Lord there?* Angus wondered. *And will he answer?* He gazed through the tangle of hay at the gray dimness of the rafters and thatch above him. He thought he detected a tiny shaft of sunlight glimmering faintly through the clouds and making its way through a gap in the thatch. His crying out to God became more fervent, and as so often happened with Angus, his prayer shaped itself into verse:

O Jesus, King, Deliverer,
Just Sovereign, Lord, our Savior,
Increase my faith; make strong thy arm;
O God, free us from hell's alarm.

Another slicing thrust of the blade—and another clunk, this against hard-packed earth. The trooper had to be close now. Angus listened: the heavy tread of boots on the floor; another thrust, another harmless clunk of blade. If only Angus could do something. Never had he felt so helpless. Each relentless tread, each cruel thrust could mean death for his father. He couldn't just let the brute run him through. No, he *wouldn't* let him do it.

He felt for his bow. How much time would it take him to tear off the hay, set an arrow on the string, draw his bow, aim, and fire? But would he be hopelessly tangled in hay so that he couldn't shoot? Well, it didn't matter, now. He would do what he could. Angus grabbed up an armful of hay ready to throw it off—

But wait! He strained his ears to listen. The soldier halted, but he made no thrust. Maybe the young man spotted his father and was even at that moment raising his sword in both hands, a cruel grin spreading across his face, and taking careful aim before plunging his blade into the fugitive.

But nothing happened. Angus held his breath. If the man shouted, he'd bring the whole murdering troop down on Angus's father—and on Angus.

"Lie still!"

Angus couldn't believe his ears. "Lie still!" It was the soldier's voice in a husky whisper.

"Hide yerself better under the straw, man," the soldier said urgently. "I, for one, will not discover ye. Are there more of ye, man?"

"Only my lad, in the loft," came his father's whispered voice.

"Ye there, young Boig!" Claverhouse's voice boomed from the yard. "What hae ye found?"

"No living thing, yer lairdship," called back Boig, hacking fiercely at the hay.

Then, Boig moved throughout the barn, flailing loudly at the hay with his sword.

Angus shook his head in bewilderment. This young officer, a soldier in the service of the king and of bloody Claverhouse, had spared their lives, and at great risk to himself. He was a Royalist, an Anglican. How could this be?

"There's nothing in the house, yer lairdship," a soldier called.

"Och, the traitors somehow got word of our coming," growled another.

"Foul Whigs," said one. "Hanging's too good for the lot of 'em."

Without a word, the dragoon called Boig turned on his heel and made for the yard.

"All right men, fire the house," ordered Claverhouse, "then lend a blade to Boig in the barn. We'll hack it up and burn it to the ground."

Angus felt his heart skip a beat. Fire the barn—with them in it?

"My blade returns thirsty," called Boig. "I've hacked the pathetic hay to bits. The old man and his wife must be miles away."

"Well, then," said Claverhouse, "burn it to the ground."

21 FIRE!

At that moment, the only death Angus could imagine to be worse than death by random sword thrust in the hay—was burning alive in a barn. His scalp crawled as he heard the striking of a flint and then the roaring of flames as the dry thatch on the Blantyres' croft caught fire.

Would he and his father stay in the barn and be burned alive, or run for it and be shot as they fled. It was doubtful that he would have time to shoot his bow before the dragoons fired. And, swordsman that he was, could his father take on six armed men?

"Looks like rain, yer lairdship," Angus heard Boig's voice above the crackling of the fire.

"Aye, but ye'll not want to be missing out on the show," replied Claverhouse.

"Firing an empty house and barn, if yer lairdship will forgive me for saying it," said Boig, "doesnae sound to me like much of a show."

He's trying to draw Claverhouse away so we can escape, thought Angus in wonder. *All this, and the man doesnae even ken us.*

"Men, Corporal Boig here will fire the barn," said Claverhouse. "Take up the torch, Boig."

He suspects, thought Angus. *Claverhouse suspects something. So he's making Boig do it. But will he do it?*

"Angus, get down here!" his father's voice hissed above the rushing of the fire rapidly consuming the roof of the nearby croft. "With this rising wind, our man Boig won't need to light the barn. It'll ignite on its own from the house."

"What are we going to do, Father?" asked Angus.

"Pray for rain, and lots of it. But we'll dig while we pray, lad."

They rushed to the back of the barn, and his father fell to his knees and began jabbing his claymore in the packed earth at the base of the stone wall. Angus dug with his dirk and frantically scrapped the clods of loose earth away with his hands.

Rushing wind and the roaring and crackling of flames sounded above them in the thatch. Within minutes, wads of flaming heather thatch fell like missiles from the roof onto the dry straw all around them. Smoke tore at Angus's throat. He could barely breathe, and tears streamed down his face as he stomped and flailed his plaid at the nearest flames.

"Grab that rake!" said his father. "Clear away the burning hay from the floor! Rake it to the front of the barn." With a savage thrust of his sword, his father turned back to the growing hole. "I'm nearly through."

Then, above the flames, Angus heard Claverhouse bellow. "Prime yer muskets, lads. Surround the barn. We wouldnae want any Whigs finding another way out, now would we, Corporal Boig?"

They heard the muffled sound of horses' hooves on the other side of the wall.

"What now?" gasped Angus. With a crack, a rafter near the front of the barn gave way under the flames and fell into the hayloft where Angus had hidden. Flames leapt higher.

"We keep digging," said his father, coughing. "Horses

won't last long in the lee of this smoke. While there's hope, we keep digging."

The hole grew larger. "Angus, if we can lever out this stone, we'll both be through." His father pried with his claymore at a large stone, now loose and undermined by their digging.

"But the dragoons," cried Angus, throwing his weight against the stone. "They're waiting for us."

"Aye, with billows of smoke in their eyes, lad. And listen to their horses."

Through the opening Angus could hear the stomping and screaming of the horses as the men tried to keep them at their post on the leeward side of the fire.

His father stuck his head cautiously out the hole.

"As I'd hoped. They're backing away up the hill to try to get clear of the smoke. From uphill, all they'll see of this side of the barn is black smoke. Now, then, Angus, one last heave and we're free."

"But where can we run to? They'll see us for sure—and shoot us dead!"

"One thing at a time, lad. Now, heave!"

The stone gave way. Angus's father threw his claymore and musket out ahead of him, squirmed his way through the opening, and lay flat. Angus tossed his bow through the hole and followed. Relieved as he was to get out of the flaming barn, he feared what awaited them at the hands of Claverhouse and his dragoons. These men were thorough at their business.

At a signal from his father, Angus helped roll the stone back in place, and under cover of smoke they packed earth in the cracks around it.

"If they think we've escaped, they'll scour the countryside till they find us," his father explained in a whisper.

"Now we make for the well," his father hissed in his ear. "The smoke won't descend into it, and we should have enough air to breathe in the well shaft—at least for a while."

Angus and his father crawled on their bellies, the smoke churning in the air above them, until they reached the well. Angus's father stood up and threw his leg over the stone sill. Angus watched as his father leaned his back against one side and, using counter pressure with his feet against the other, lowered himself fifteen feet down into the darkness of the well shaft. Angus followed. They halted just above the water level and waited.

The wind died down and a drizzling of rain fell. Angus's legs began to shimmy and tingle from the strain of the continual counter pressure needed to hold himself up against the inside of the well. Would he have strength enough to climb out? They saw less and less smoke drifting in the circle of light above them. The rain must be extinguishing the flames. But would Claverhouse just ride off and leave them? As they waited, his father began disassembling both of his pistols. Handing one of the barrels to Angus, he signaled for silence.

"Are they gone?" mouthed Angus.

His father held his finger to his lips and shook his head.

"I feel it in my bones," came Claverhouse's gravelly voice, faint at first, but growing louder as he spoke. "I smell 'em in the mist. There's Whigs about. And I want them. Search the entire area. Boig, ye come with me. I'll teach ye how to root out Presbyterians."

Angus's father pointed down and lowered himself into the cold well water. Grimacing from the stiffness in his legs, Angus followed. His father put the pistol barrel to his lips, and silently, with one hand on the wet stone wall, he lowered himself, head and all, into the water, his barrel just poking above the surface. Angus heard his steady breathing through the barrel. His father surfaced slowly and grinned.

"This way, Boig," barked Claverhouse, sounding nearer. "Muskets at the ready. These vermin can show from time to time a cleverness above their station. Be on the alert."

His jaw tense, Angus's father looked steadily up at the well opening. Claverhouse came closer.

"Och, the well," said Claverhouse.

"The well, sir?" said Boig.

"Aye, Boig. Check the well," ordered Claverhouse.

Angus and his father heard the horses' breath amplified into great draws and blows above them.

His father pointed down and set the barrel to his lips. Angus felt a rising panic as he put the barrel in his mouth and lowered his head into the water. Eyes squinted tightly shut, he drew a breath. It tasted of oil and gunpowder, but he could breathe. Underwater, the voices and snorting of the horses popped strangely in his ears. What if they saw them? Would Claverhouse just shoot them? They had no means of defense. His father's powder was all ruined by the water, and the well shaft was too narrow for him to shoot his bow. He had an almost uncontrollable urge to lift his head and see what was about to happen. Claverhouse would discover them for sure if he did. But how long could they wait?

After what seemed like hours, his father tugged on his arm, and Angus heard him surface. Bracing himself for what he might see, Angus rose cautiously to the surface.

Up to their necks in water, father and son waited, every nerve taut, their ears straining to hear through the rain.

"*They* might keep quiet for so long," whispered his father, "but surely their horses couldnae. Follow me, Angus."

After peering cautiously over the sill of the well, they clamored out and collapsed on the wet ground. Looking numbly around at the smoldering remains of the farm, and too weary to speak, they helped each other to their feet and turned their steps toward home.

As they trudged along the moor, Angus felt a rising in his soul as he watched the late afternoon sun break through the clouds and cast its amber light across the heather. He couldn't remember seeing anything so beautiful. Halting in his tracks, his father raised his face heavenward and lifted his great hands.

> "O Praise the Lord, for he is good;
> His mercy lasteth ever.
> Let those of Israel now say,
> His mercy faileth never."

Mary M'Kethe and Jennie walked anxiously back and forth along the little fortified wall, their eyes searching the moor. Angus and his father had been away too long. They heard them before they saw them, father and son singing, almost shouting their praises over the moor:

> "I in distress called on the Lord;
> The Lord did answer me:
> He in a large place did me set,
> From trouble made me free."

As Angus and his father came into view, the women saw faces and hands blackened by soot, and hair and cloths singed and frayed by the flames. But their singing grew louder.

"The mighty Lord is on my side,
  I will not be afraid;
For anything that man can do
  I shall not be dismayed.
Thou art my God, I'll thee exalt;
  My God I will thee praise.
Give thanks to God, for he is good:
  His mercy lasts always."

That night around the hearth Angus and his father told the whole story of their deliverance, Malcolm acting out his favorite parts and urging them to tell it over and over again. And like Celtic bards long ages before him, Angus turned the story into verse and sang it to the rapt attention of his family. He finally concluded with the lines:

. . . O Jesus, King, Deliverer,
Just Sovereign, Lord, our Savior,
When cruel flames around us leapt,
Closing in foul Claverhouse crept,
Our God arose with power and might
And set our bloody foe to flight.
All praise sweet King, Deliverer,
Just Sovereign, Lord our Savior!

When the last chanting strains of the tale died away, with a squeal, Malcolm jumped to his feet and began dancing an ancient victory fling before the fire.

"It grows late," laughed Sandy M'Kethe, sweeping up his

grandson in his arms. “And tomorrow is the Sabbath. Let’s away to our beds with grateful hearts.”

When the house was finally quiet, Angus stared into the smoldering peat and said, “Father, I would like someday to meet Corporal Boig.”

“Perhaps someday ye shall,” his father replied. “But for now, lad, get some rest. Tomorrow is the Sabbath. We worship at Drumclog.”

22
SABBATH AT DRUMCLOG
(June 1, 1679)

Blue sky and warm sunlight shone overhead next morning, but doubt and fear clouded the minds of many worshipers. They knew that while Covenanters worshiped on the Sabbath, Claverhouse was at his bloody work on the Sabbath, and all the more after the recent troubles. Nevertheless, the M'Kethes and many of their neighbors determined to assemble in the Lord's name. After an early morning tramp down the moor, they arrived at the trysting place.

Rising above the mosshags and bogs surrounding Drumclog, the deep clear voice of Mr. Thomas Douglas called the congregation to worship.

"Our great Redeemer has spread for us a table in the wilderness, and most worthy is the Lamb that was slain to receive from our lips the highest praise and the deepest gratitude."

Angus looked around at the large gathering. There must be more than two hundred. There were women casting anxious glances at the hills while holding nursing babies protectively in their arms, and there were children of every age. Here and there stood a stooped elderly couple, and there were the Blantyres. The old man's white hair quavered in the breeze, and he grasped his bonnet in his hand. And there were able-bodied men, who against the king's decree, came to worship with weapons in hand. Many, like Angus's father and Duncan and Jamie, carried muskets, swords, and pistols. Others carried pitchforks, homemade pikes, scythes. One or two carried heavy clubs made from tree branches. Angus carried his bow. William Cleland; Henry Hall of Haugh-head; Sir Robert Hamilton; David Hackston; poor William Dingwall; John Campbell, Earl of Loudoun; Thomas Fleming, tenant of the earl; the Lord of Torfoot; and John Burly Balfour and others came to worship heavily armed.

The hills echoed with their singing. "O thou my soul, bless God the Lord, and all that in me is . . ."

"Hear the Word of the Lord," called Mr. Douglas when they finished singing. " 'It is better to take refuge in the Lord than to trust in princes.' "

The fugitive minister read on. Angus stole a glance at the earl. What had the earl's father said long ago before the king? Something about Church and state being distinct, but also that justice and religion cannot exist without each other, and so the Church and the state—how did he say it?—"must stand and fall, live and die together." In these times, reflected Angus, it seemed more like dying than living. In any case, there was certainly not much temptation to trust in princes with Charles on the throne.

Mr. Douglas's voice continued. "They surrounded me on every side, but in the name of the Lord I cut them off. They swarmed around me like bees—"

Suddenly, from a ridge above the morass of Drumclog a single musket shot cracked. Mr. Douglas halted midsentence, and anxious eyes scanned the hills. A puff of smoke lingered on the ridge. Flailing his arms wildly, the sentinel ran down the slope toward the meeting place.

"Bloody Claverhouse!" he called breathlessly. "And some forty dragoons and soldiers of foot, too."

"Aye, then, ye've got the theory," said Mr. Douglas, his big Bible closing with a thump. "Now for the practice."

"To arms!" yelled John Burly Balfour. "O, my country would bless my memory could my sword this day give Claverhouse's villainous carcass to the crows!"

"Who leads us?" asked the earl of Loudoun. "We cannae just throw ourselves at the marauding monster and hope for the best."

"The lands of Drumclog belong to the Hamiltons," said Sandy M'Kethe. "If we are to protect our families this day and gain the victory, we must make good use of these peat hags and swamps here about. And no one kens these bogs and mosshags better than a Hamilton."

"Will ye accept the command, Sir Robert?" asked Mr. Douglas.

"If God and his people wish it," said Hamilton. "I accept it."

***

Meanwhile, determined to apprehend the Rutherglen protesters, Claverhouse with some one hundred fifty soldiers had been on the prowl since early morning. Unbeknownst to the Drumclog worshipers, he had already that day dispersed a Sabbath gathering near Galashiels and had seized the women, including several ladies of noble birth, and had the faithful minister Thomas Wilkie in his maw. Not satisfied, just north of Drumclog near the village of Hamilton, the commander broke up a conventicle led by the kindly Mr. John King. Claverhouse bound Mr. King and fourteen other worshipers and dragged them along behind his troops like cattle. Only a few miles away, near Strathaven Castle, Claverhouse was informed of a large conventicle gathered near Loudoun Hill on the lands of Andrew Hamilton, Lord of Drumclog. Dragging Mr. King and his exhausted prisoners behind the horses, Claverhouse threatened to court-martial any of his men who didn't give their all in crushing this "rendezvous of rebellion."

After eight miles of impatient riding, Loudoun Hill rose out of rolling pastureland on Claverhouse's left, and Hamilton's land—Drumclog—lay just before them. Claverhouse rode to the top of a ridge and surveyed the countryside. He saw a puff of blue smoke spurt from the next ridge, and an instant later he heard the retort of a musket. They'd been spotted by a sentinel.

"To arms, men," said Claverhouse, adjusting his lace sleeves. "We shall have Whig stew for supper. Drive on those prisoners. We advance."

"If ye'll be forgiving me for saying so, yer Lairdship," said one of his men. "But the prisoners are all clouts and bloodied from doing their best to keep up with horses. I ken some'll die if we drive them any farther."

"Och, ye donnae ken nothing, Corporal!" barked Claverhouse, his face growing red with rage. "It's my business, the killing of Whigs. It's what I do. So why should I care if these prisoners are all clouts and bloodied? Drive them on, man. We advance."

***

"What weapons and what fighting men of foot and of horse have we?" yelled Hamilton.

"Forty men of horse," cried William Cleland. "And fifty of foot who bear what can be considered weapons. O that we had Cameron and Cargill here with us today."

Angus strung his bow and frowned. Had William counted him among the fifty?

"Angus, help me get the women and children and the aged to safety up the moor," called his father.

"O, do keep us near to hand, Sandy," said Mary M'Kethe, Jennie's arm looped in her mother's. "We'll be needed to render aid to the wounded."

Angus slung his bow over his shoulder and scooped up the twins, one in each arm. He hoped there'd be no wounded that day. Fiona gathered up her skirts and cooed encouraging words to the terrified children as she followed Angus to safety. Lindsay kept a firm grip on Malcolm, who kept twisting around eager to watch the men form themselves into ranks and prepare for battle.

"Here he comes!" called Malcolm, breaking free from his mother's grasp for an instant. He raised his little fists and took a defiant leap into the air, then landed with a squashing sound in the bog. "It's bloody Claverhouse! Get 'im, Father! Grandfather! Get 'im!"

"Och, lad, they cannae fault ye for yer zeal," said Lindsay, yanking him to his feet. "But this is real, and ye're too young to go plunging into the fray just now. Yer task is to watch and pray with yer mother. And may God preserve our own."

Angus set the twins down and made sure that Fiona and Lindsay were out of range of the fighting. He felt a twinge inside his mind. Somehow it didn't seem right just then for him to feel passed over by his nephew. Why hadn't Malcolm cried, "Get 'im, Angus!" He scowled at himself in frustration. Here they all were on the verge of a great battle where some would live victorious—and others would die vanquished, and here he was feeling sorry for himself. He shook his head violently, as if trying to shake off some loathsome monster clutching at his mind.

"Flee over the moor—if ye must. Flee like the wind," he said to Fiona and Lindsay. "And God be with ye."

From the rising ground where Angus had led the women and children and the aged, he watched the white plume of Claverhouse's helmet jostle as he led his men down the opposite slope. The soldiers pouring down the hillside made Angus think of bright red apples tumbling out of a barrel, only here sun flashed menacingly on armor and weapons. Then, he spotted Mr. King and the prisoners, bound and staggering behind the horses. They looked exhausted, their faces bruised and blood smeared, and their clothes hung about them in tatters from numerous stumblings and draggings.

Then to the right, Angus watched as Sir Robert Hamilton formed the footmen into three ranks in the center of their position, brave Hackston and Henry Hall commanding. A small company of well-armed men of horse he divided and placed on either side of the impromptu infantry. Burly Balfour led one of these companies. And it looked as though young William Cleland was being given the command of the middle rank of foot soldiers, including Angus's father and brothers. *William looks so gallant and brave*, Angus thought, *like he is eager for the rumble of muskets and the hacking and slashing of claymores*. On the right flank, Angus watched the Lord of Torfoot inspect his small but determined troop of cavalry.

And here I am guarding the women and children, thought Angus bitterly as he heard behind him the quavering voices of women and the lisping tremor of children as old John Blantyre led them in singing a psalm full of words of hope and confidence in the God of Jacob.

Something was happening in the enemy's ranks. Angus watched Claverhouse make a cleaving stroke at the air with his sword and order a halt. Then, over the mosshags and hillocks of Drumclog thundered the defiant rolling of the king's kettledrums. The swelling rumbling sent an ominous chill up Angus's spine. Then, with a nod from Claverhouse, a single dragoon captain, a banner of truce fluttering in the breeze above him, trotted toward Hamilton for a parley.

What is Claverhouse up to? Angus wondered in amazement. *Is he suing for peace? Has he seen our strength and now wants to surrender? Can a wolf become a lamb? No, surely not this wolf.*

Fingering the feathers of an arrow, Angus surveyed the scene unfolding before him. He glanced at the sky. A growing number of crows circled, dipping and gliding expectantly overhead. They seemed to know that battle meant food, easy pickings and lots of it.

In revulsion he tore his eyes from the crows. If he only knew what Claverhouse was up to. He studied the ridge that bordered the king's bloody commander and his army. With a quickening of his pulse, an idea began forming in his mind. If he crept around to the northwest, the ridge would conceal him from sight. He might just be able to get a closer look at Claverhouse's strength and, if he was careful, listen in.

From the hillock he looked down at where his father and Duncan and Jamie fell in formation in the middle ranks of the battlefield. There was no time to consult his father, he thought with anguish, but the information he might gather could be the difference between winning the battle—or being crushed under the heel of bloody Claverhouse. He glanced back at the band of women and children huddled together on the moor. A tremor ran throughout his body as he thought of what Claverhouse would do to his mother, to Jennie and the children after he'd slaughtered all the men—Angus had heard. He looked back at Claverhouse, whose breastplate glittered in the sun, and the white plume atop his helm waved defiantly in the breeze. Angus tried to swallow. His throat felt dry as oat straw before the rains fell. What would Claverhouse do to a spy?

Then, with a set to his jaw and a firm grip on his bow, he bent low and disappeared over the ridge, making his way directly toward the muskets and swords of Claverhouse's dragoons.

Angus's heart thundered in his ears as he ran, and his breath came in deep gulps and in heaving gasps. Was it fear? From over the ridge, but still unseen, he heard the clanking of enemy swords, the neighing and clomping of restless horses, the hollering of men preparing for battle, all drifting ominously over the ridge. Louder and louder it grew with every stride.

Glancing at the thin green line of the ridge just above him, Angus realized with a sinking in his breast that if Claverhouse sent a patrol a few yards up from the other side of that ridge—Angus would have nowhere to hide. He'd be captured in an instant. He'd heard what would happen after that.

He threw himself flat into the heather, his breath knocked from his heaving lungs as when a piper finishes his piping and the cow-stomach bag deflates with a chirrup and a wheeze. When he could breathe again, he slithered on his belly through the heather toward the ridge. Every clink of steel, every snort of horse, every shout, and Angus was certain he was discovered. But still he crept nearer the ridge. So close was he now that it seemed he could hear the very breathing of Claverhouse and his cruel soldiers. He imagined he could hear the officers' hearts beating like great gongs inside their breastplates.

Burrowing into the springy tangle of a clump of heather atop the ridge, Angus slowly parted the prickly branches. His heart nearly stopped. Claverhouse! Surrounded by row upon row of infantry, muskets primed, and cavalry—men and horse—champing, straining to descend on the worshipers-turned-army clearly visible across the morass. So near were the soldiers he felt he could reach down and touch the closest men.

Then amidst a flurry of pounding hooves, the officer sent to parley reined in next to Claverhouse. *What had they said?* Angus wondered.

"Foul Whigs, your Lairdship!" called the envoy breathlessly. "They'll not bow. Nor will they turn over the traitors who've gone and organized this offensive rebellion against the king—and against your Lairdship."

"So I hoped," snarled Claverhouse. Men laughed. "Their blood be on their own heads. Be it 'No quarters' this day. We'll leave none of them alive at their own request. And that includes their shrieking women and bairns. 'No quarters,' men. We bathe these mosshags in red this day."

"And the prisoners?" said one from Claverhouse's left.

"The prisoners, Corporal," replied Claverhouse in a mocking tone, "should they offer to run away—must be shot through the head. Food for the crows. It would save us the bother of feeding them only to end their miserable lives later on."

Mr. King and the prisoners had collapsed in exhaustion and, still chained to one another, lay on the moor.

Claverhouse drew his sword and pointed at three of his men.

"You three will guard the vermin. Now get them out of my sight. Prepare to charge, and let the word be 'No quarters!' None shall live, err we sheathe our weapons this day."

Three dragoons yanked on the prisoners' bonds and led them to the left of the battle lines. Mr. King and three or four others stumbled to their knees in weariness.

"And in the unlikely event," called Claverhouse over his shoulder, "that ye three are needed in the battle—cut the prisoners' throats."

Angus heard a weary groan from the band of prisoners.

How many miles had they been dragged that day? And now so little hope. If Claverhouse wins the day, they die at the gallows in Glasgow. If the Covenanters win, they die at the hands of their guards. If only he could do something to free them.

"We attack their middle ranks," barked Claverhouse. "They're mere rabble with pitchforks. Then our cavalry pours in on the flanks. We wash our hands in their blood, and so ends another day's loyal service to the king."

Angus slithered backwards until clear of the ridge and then ran like the wind to rejoin his father and the defenders.

As breathless he neared the Covenanting ranks, he heard the men singing Psalm 76 to the mournful tune "Martyrs," its mysterious loveliness filling the bogs and mosshags and rising in strength to the hillocks of Drumclog.

"In Judah's land God is well known,
His name's in Israel great . . ."

Angus felt a thrill of hope rising in his soul. As he ran the last few yards and the grandeur of the ancient lyric surrounded him, he found himself singing with the men.

"Their arrows of the bow he brake,
The shield, the sword, the war.
More glorious Thou than hills of prey,
More excellent art far."

As the final strains of the psalm died in the breeze, Angus shouldered his way through the men until he found his father.

"Where have ye been, lad? We've worried ourselves to distraction about ye."

"Father, I stole close in to Clavers and his ranks."

"Ye did what?"

"Aye, that wee ridge concealing me, I stole up close and heard all."

"What did ye hear?—no, wait. The battle's nearly joined. Ye'll speak it once."

And with that, Angus's father led him to Sir Robert Hamilton.

"My lad, here, has information, sir," he said. "Tell all, Angus."

Angus tried to reconstruct exactly what he'd heard.

"Women and bairns, too?" said Angus's father when all was told.

"And ye're sure about cutting the throats of the prisoners?" Sir Robert pressed Angus.

"Aye, 'tis what he ordered," replied Angus. "And he ordered, 'Be it no quarters. All will die.' "

"I hae no quarrel with 'No quarters,' " said Sir Robert. "We too can fight by Claverhouse's rule of no quarter given to prisoners or those fleeing the field." Then looking severely at Angus, he continued. "Now then, lad, are ye sure about the middle ranks and the flanking of their cavalry? Are ye certain?"

"So said Claverhouse, sir," replied Angus.

"Sir Robert!" cried William Cleland from the left rank of the cavalry. "Clavers comes on! He orders a volley!"

23 FIRST BLOOD AT DRUMCLOG

Clavers signals his men to fire!" shouted William Cleland.

"So he does!" cried Hamilton, his gaze fixed on Claverhouse's raised sword, and the enemy's foot soldiers, their muskets at the ready.

"Fall to the heather!" cried young Cleland from his place at the head of the foot soldiers. Claverhouse's sword came down in a viscious signal.

A deafening roar erupted from the enemy's guns. Angus and his father along with the entire company of Covenanters fell facedown in the sod, searing lead ball whistling through the air less than a yard above their prone bodies.

Angus shuddered with dread as he imagined what lead ball tearing into his chest would feel like. Had any of theirs been hit? How many? He listened for the groans of the dying.

"On yer feet, men!" yelled Hamilton, moving from rank to rank. "They've struck not a one of us, lads. Take heart. God is on our side. Prepare for their charge. Prime yer muskets!"

Angus swallowed a dry lump forming in his throat as he watched the line where Claverhouse was arrayed. Swords aloft. The men who had just fired the first volley came

Battle at Drumclog

pouring down the hillock like a red-coated wave, yelling in defiance.

"No quarters! No quarters!" they cried.

"Steady men." Hamilton's voice was calm and firm. "We donnae have extra powder, lads. Let them come closer."

Closer? Angus watched in horror as the redcoats neared. He could see their features now. There was a man with a scar on his left cheek; and another with a large nose; still another with deep blue eyes, red hair just showing under his helmet. As ominous as they were collectively, as battle hungry as most of them appeared, Angus was sure he detected fear in the wide eyes of one, and a look on another's face that told of the deepest reluctance. Angus watched Claverhouse order his next

line of infantry to advance and ready themselves for a volley. *We'll be overrun*, thought Angus. *They're too close*.

"Present and give fire!" ordered Hamilton.

Just as Duncan and Jamie and the first line of men of foot discharged their muskets, Angus watched some of Claverhouse's charging men suddenly stumble and fall with a splat facedown into the swampy ditch that divided the armies, musket balls whizzing harmlessly over their heads, while still other men fell in agony clutching their chests where musket balls had found their mark. The bog spared not a few of the king's men in that first charge, who, besmeared with mud, dragged themselves to their feet and staggered back to their ranks.

Another volley from Claverhouse; another charge repulsed by the defenders of the Kirk. All around him men poured powder, rammed wadding, loaded lead ball, and primed their muskets. The air was heavy with the acrid stench of saltpeter. Tears flowed from Angus's eyes, and he was sure it was from the smoky air. And still Claverhouse's men fired volley after volley and came on.

While his father and Duncan and Jamie fired their muskets, Angus loaded their pistols. But the battle had not been engaged for long before it was clear to Angus that Claverhouse's men loaded and discharged their weapons much faster. Hamilton and his men carried obsolete muskets, relics of another time, and Claverhouse had trained his men well in their bloody work. Armed only with superior convictions, how long could the defenders hold out against the far better muskets and firepower of the king's men?

Next Claverhouse ordered a cavalry charge. More terrifying than the men of foot, horses thundered down the hill, and men shrieked with swords drawn, all thirsty for blood. Angus tried to suppress the rising terror he felt as the horses and men came on. Closer and still closer came the pounding of hooves and the defiant cries of the men, until it seemed to Angus that nothing could stop them. Then, the pounding of hooves turned to a sucking and slogging sound. And the defenders shouted with joy as the first line of cavalry foundered in the boggy ditch. Horses screamed and fell, and their men catapulted forward squelching into the mire. Some of the king's men tried to turn their mounts and retreat but were cut down by a volley from the defenders.

Then, above the clamor and shouting of the battle, from the direction of Loudoun Hill, came a trumpet blast. Angus strained to see. Highlanders descending to reinforce Claverhouse? More redcoats? But no.

Spurring their horses fiercely, their claymores circling defiantly overhead, Captain John Nisbet and one other man came on to join the fray. Nisbet reined in near John Balfour.

"Jump the ditch and charge the enemy!" he cried.

"For God and Country!" shouted Nisbet, burying his heels in his horse's flanks. The men took up the cry as they charged across the morass. "For God and Country!"

"What are ye doing here!" In the midst of all, Angus heard his father cry and spun to look. His mother and Jennie had made their way toward the middle of the Covenanting ranks.

"We'll be needed for the wounded," his mother explained as calmly as she could, though there was a tremor in her reply.

"Ye'll be *among* the wounded, dear Mary," cried Sandy M'Kethe, gripping his wife by the shoulders. "Ye must stay back. Follow at our rear and from there tend the wounded and dying. And may God be with ye both."

The women retreated to the relative safety of the back lines. Angus loaded a pistol as they surged forward. He handed it to his father and began loading his father's musket.

So much confusion surrounded them. On every side, the chaos of yelling and screaming men, many yelling in defiance, some screaming in agony and terror. Flashes of the struggle bit hauntingly into Angus's mind, never to be dislodged: the ringing clang of a sword struck from an exhausted hand; the pleading horror of the eyes; the quaking hands lifted in desperate but futile defense; the babbling scream as the stroke descended; the sickening, tearing sound of the claymore as it cleaved flesh and bone; the blood; the crumpled body; the lifeless, gazing eyes.

Is God on our side? Angus wondered numbly as he passed his father the loaded musket. Is God fighting for us? Are we winning the day?

They surged forward. His father drew his claymore. The

cries of the men all around him sounded louder and more jubilant.

"God's enemies are my enemies!" he heard one cry near them. "And praise be to God, he's scattered them before us!"

"For God and Country!" rang across the field.

Then with horror, Angus remembered the prisoners. What will become of the prisoners? He grabbed his father's arm.

"But what of Mr. King and the prisoners?" shouted Angus in his ear. He felt a wrenching foreboding in his stomach. "Claverhouse ordered their throats cut if the battle went against the king!"

24 LET FLY IN THE NAME OF GOD!

"'Cut their throats,'" recited Angus, looking desperately into his father's eyes, "'if the battle goes against us'—or words like it, so said Claverhouse."

"So he did, lad." His father halted, looking about the field. "And God is giving us victory over his enemies this day."

"But they'll cut their throats," said Angus, choking on the words.

"Aye they will," said his father, taking Angus's shoulders in his hands and looking intently into his son's eyes. "Angus, ye must run like the wind and free worthy Mr. King and the rest. I'd not trust any man with a musket to do it without killing some of our own. But ye can do it with yer bow."

"Free them, Father? With my bow?"

"Aye, free them with yer bow. Ye're little help here with the claymore, but ye can free them with yer bow, lad, and ye must. Clavers' men must be stopped from murdering worthy Mr. King and the rest." He stroked Angus's hair. "And ye alone can stop them if ye run like the wind and yer aim is true. Now be off with ye. And, Angus, let fly in the name of God."

Angus turned to the ridge and ran. His father had just ordered him to go and kill three men. And Sir Robert Hamilton, the commander, had ordered them to take no prisoners, to spare not one of God's enemies that day. Angus tried to get his mind to work, to understand what was right. But all he could think was that his peace-loving father had just sent him to kill three men—in the name of God.

The wild cry of 'No quarters!' sounded from Claverhouse and his men as they came on for a final charge. Angus ran uphill until his lungs burned and his heart pounded like the blows of a blacksmith's hammer on red-hot iron.

Below, the two armies met with a grinding clash across the swamps of Drumclog. Angus had to catch his breath. He saw Claverhouse bestride his black charger, *Satan*, surrounded by a square of his men, fighting desperately to protect their commander. Nisbet, Balfour, and Cleland encircled the square of men. It looked like Claverhouse might be taken. Lord Torfoot and his cavalry descended on the right flank of the king's men. Claverhouse seemed to dart from one bog of the bloody field to another, and still his men surrounded him, and still the defenders came on like a fury. Then Angus watched in horror as Thomas Fleming, his mighty pike still clutched in his grip, fell to the mud near Claverhouse's horse. Fleming would be a great loss. Though small comfort, from where Angus ran high atop the ridge, it was clear that far more red-coated bodies lay lifeless across the morass of the battlefield.

If the prisoners' guards see this rout, moaned Angus, *I might be too late*. He ran on.

At last he collapsed to the ground on the ridge. From here he hoped to get the best sight of Mr. King and the prisoners. Seventy-five yards away the three guards seemed to be in a frenzy of panic over the situation. Several of the bound prisoners yanked violently on their bonds. *They're about to do it*, Angus realized with horror. He reached up and felt his own pulse pounding away in his neck. *They're going to cut their throats—Mr. King's throat!*

Angus selected three of his best arrows and jabbed them into the peat sod at his feet. One of the soldiers suddenly drew his sword and dagger, while the other two primed pistols. Sweat poured into Angus's eyes and he wiped it away with his sleeve. He would need to see as clearly as ever. If he missed, he might kill one of the prisoners, and his stray arrow would surely alert the soldiers to his whereabouts—and all would be lost. They'd quickly kill the prisoners—and come after him. But which of the three to shoot first?

The soldier with the drawn claymore seemed to be waiting for the men to ready their pistols. Four pistols, a sword and a dagger: six Covenanters would be dead if Angus missed. One of them might be Mr. King. And then the soldiers would resort to swords and knives to finish their bloody work.

The tallest soldier readied his pistols and strode toward the first prisoner. He wore a steel breastplate, which limited the target area. Angus's aim had to be true. He wiped his eyes, set his arrow on the string, drew, aimed at the man's neck, and let fly—in the name of God, as his father had said.

The man spun on his booted heel with a look of agony and bewildered horror. He groped at his neck for a fleeting instant and fell. The other two men stared in disbelief. Their captain had fallen, but they'd heard no musket fired; stranger still, an arrow protruded from his neck.

While they still didn't know where he was, Angus knew he had to follow up his advantage. He drew his bow. These two would be easier than the first: that lifeless redcoat had been the first man Angus had ever killed. And without breastplates these men both presented a larger target. He felt a tremor in his hand as he held the second arrow in place. What he had just done began to sink in, and he knew that he was about to end the life of another human being. That knowledge was almost more than he could bear. "Love yer enemies," Christ had said, and his father had taught him. But it was the life of these three men—or the life of the faithful minister, Angus's friend, Mr. King, and all the rest, whose only crime was worshiping God on the Sabbath.

Both soldiers began frantically scanning the ridge. They'd spot him in an instant. Angus narrowed his eyes, aimed for the breast and let fly—also in the name of God, as his father had instructed him.

The second soldier fell without a tremor and lay dead on the moor, an arrow jutting from his chest.

By this time the prisoners also turned this way and that, straining to see the source of their deliverance. The third soldier looked from his captain to his fellow soldier, both lying dead on the sod. He threw down his pistol. Then, with roving eyes and terrified twistings of his head, he turned and ran for his life.

Angus already had an arrow on the string. He drew and aimed at the fleeing soldier's back. It was a strong back, a broad back, an easy shot, and frequent stumblings in the swampy ground gave many opportunities for hitting a non-moving target, if Angus preferred that. An easy shot, indeed. But Angus somehow could not let fly. His father had told him to "let fly—in the name of God." He wasn't sure that he could do it "in the name of God." It was as if his three fingers were welded to the string. After all, the man no longer posed a threat to Mr. King and the prisoners. Nor was he running to join those still fighting against the faithful. How could he shoot him—kill him?

Angus released the string slowly and lowered his bow. The man disappeared over a hillock.

Angus slumped to the ground. He felt very tired, yet at the

same time his mind worked on what had just happened—what he had just done, or failed to do. The order from Sir Robert had been to grant no quarter—even to those fleeing the field. This was war, and Angus had just disobeyed an order. What would his father say? He knew that his father would say something that would sound very much like it came from the Bible, maybe from the Psalter. And Angus then would weave his father's words into verse, like a bard of old after a battle—around the hearth—when all was safe again.

We war not with mere flesh and blood,
Nor tyrant's heel or cannon rude,
But with the Fiend whose arrows keen
At sinner's souls he aims unseen.

Perhaps there is another battle going on this very day, Angus mused. His father would say there was. And he wondered just where the Fiend's arrows had been aimed that day?

But the prisoners. He rose quickly to his feet. *I've left Mr. King and the prisoners, all weary and bloodied, and still in their bonds.* He ran across the ridge and down to Mr. King.

"I kent it was Angus M'Kethe," said Mr. King with a weary smile as Angus cut his bonds. He grimaced as he rubbed his raw arms and wrists. "And I kent it for certain when I saw the fleeing soldier not struck down."

***

From the ridge, Angus and the prisoners had a perfect view of the battlefield as they joined the defenders for the final moments of the battle. Thomas Fleming of Loudoun did indeed find himself unhorsed and thick in mud, with horses' hooves trampling all about him. He glanced up to see none other than Claverhouse's horse, *Satan*, stomping the sod and looming just above. He made a great thrust at the horse's black stomach with his pike, and the disemboweled beast bolted in pain and terror. Claverhouse was fleeing! The horse soon collapsed from loss of blood and Claverhouse was given another. He buried his spurs in the flanks and fled the field, passing within earshot along the ridge.

"Will ye not tarry for the afternoon sermon?" called Mr. King after Claverhouse as they approached the field. Then with his face lifted heavenward he cried, "Glory be to God, who has graciously delivered the enemies of the Kirk into our hands this day!"

Mary M'Kethe and Jennie had plenty to do that day, but happily not as much among the sons of the Covenant. Only one, William Dingwall, died on the battlefield. Five others, including Thomas Fleming died later of their wounds. But forty of the king's men died on the field, and others were wounded. The defenders pursued the king's soldiers who fled the field in terror, and, in defiance of Hamilton's orders, prisoners were taken. Angus saw some of the victors tearing wads of redcoat cloth from the enemy dead that littered the field. They crammed the red cloth inside the basket hilts of their claymores and held them aloft with shouts of triumph.

"Angus," called his father, his fist still gripping his bloodied claymore. "Ye freed the prisoners in the name of God, I see. Now then, haste ye, Angus. Yer mother and Jennie need us."

Angus followed his father through the clutter and carnage of the battlefield, the moor grass trampled and the swampy ground running with Royalist blood. Dead horses lay strewn about the morass, and the fallen lay in muddied heaps over the field. Angus watched in horror as Burly Balfour and others dispatched with their dirks and claymores the wounded redcoats. His father halted before the broken body of a king's soldier not much older than Jennie, his head cradled on her lap, his face blanching with pain and graying from loss of blood.

"I cannae let them just slay him like a dog," she cried, her eyes darting from the man's face to the gruesome scene of killing.

"Jennie, my dear," said their father. "Ye've a heart full of compassion, lass. Donnae ever lose that tenderness. But, Jennie, they'll not need to slay him." He reached out his strong hand and closed the man's lifeless eyes, then he laid his arm across Jennie's shoulders and helped her to her feet. "He's gone. There's nothing more ye can do here, Jennie. Now come away. Yer place is with yer mother and the bairns up the moor."

From across the battlefield a commotion of voices suddenly broke in.

"The order was quite clear: 'No quarters,' " came a familiar voice. Angus and his father turned and walked toward the men.

"It's Burly Balfour, Father," said Angus.

"Aye, and some of ours have taken prisoners," said his father, breaking into a run.

Angus ran after his father, dodging the mangled bodies of horses and men. Here and there his father leaped over the carnage in his eagerness to get to the scene.

" 'No quarters' means no prisoners taken alive," continued Balfour's gravelly voice. "This is war, men, not church." Balfour readied his pistols.

A shot rang out and one of the redcoat prisoners slumped to the ground. Angus and his father were still fifty yards away when the man fell. Balfour raised his second pistol.

"Nae! Nae!" roared Angus's father in indignation as he closed the last yards rapidly.

Angus looked at the pale faces and wide eyes of the prisoners. The shot caught the attention of others, and men gathered to the spot, including Mr. King and some of the freed Covenanter prisoners. Balfour turned when Sandy M'Kethe yelled, but he kept his pistol trained on the broad chest of the redcoat prisoner next in line. Angus watched the doomed man's face: his eyebrows rose, and a muscle in his cheek began an involuntary twitching. Something about the man's broad shoulders and the way he carried himself made Angus study him more carefully.

"Ye'll not do it, man!" Sandy M'Kethe cried, striding boldly up to Balfour. "No more of yer murdering ways besmirching the cause of Christ and the Kirk. Put down yer weapon, man."

"He's a foul persecutor of the Kirk, man!" Balfour yelled angrily. "Och, it's not murder when the order is 'No quarters.' This is no English tea party, M'Kethe. It's war."

Balfour drew back the hammer of his pistol with a click. The redcoat soldier squared his shoulders and blinked rapidly. Before Angus fully grasped what was happening, he saw his father place himself deliberately between Balfour's pistol and the king's soldier.

"Ye'll have to shoot me first," said Sandy M'Kethe, staring defiantly back at Burly Balfour.

"What!" exclaimed Balfour, his pistol now aimed at Sandy M'Kethe. "Are ye prepared to defend the enemies of the Kirk with yer own life? Think, man."

"Lead the other prisoners aside, out of earshot," ordered Sandy M'Kethe, without taking his eyes off of Balfour and his pistol. "This one stays here."

When the other soldiers were led off, Balfour, his face red with rage, lowered his gun.

"Ye've got some explaining to do, man," he said, looking narrowly at Sandy M'Kethe.

"I do." Then turning to the soldier, Sandy said, "What's yer name and rank?"

"Boig, Corporal Boig, sir," replied the man.

Angus stared wide-eyed at Boig.

"This man," said Sandy M'Kethe, deliberately, his back still to Balfour, "I say, this man saved my life and my son's."

"Och, man," said Balfour. "That might just say more about yer loyalties than his."

"Hear him out, Balfour," said Mr. King.

Angus's father then told the story of Boig's protection at the Blantyres' barn.

"When he could hae discovered us to Claverhouse," concluded Sandy M'Kethe, "he didnae." Then addressing Boig, he said, "I donnae pretend to ken why ye did what ye did for me and my lad, but I'm most grateful."

"I donnae see as this changes anything," snorted Balfour. "He's our enemy, a soldier of bloody Claverhouse the terror of the godly, and I say—he dies."

"John Burly Balfour," said Mr. King, stepping up to the man. "Ye're right in thinking that hating God's enemies is a commendable thing, so it says many a place in Holy Scripture. But, man, Christ calls us, as well, to love our enemies. By the authority of God's Word, I say ye're confusing things. When ye should be loving yer enemy—this man, Corporal Boig—ye're hating instead.

"There's another thing," continued Mr. King. "This man did all he could to contain the cruelties of Claverhouse when we prisoners were driven on. He spoke up to slow the pace; he suggested easier routes when we were on the march; he gave more than one of us a swallow of cool water from his own drinking flask. I'm wondering if he *is* our enemy after all."

"Humph! Look at his coat," said Balfour.

"The Lord kens I hate bloody Claverhouse's ways," said Boig, his voice tense, "and his cause."

"Why march with him then and wear the coat of the king's dragoons?" demanded Balfour.

"Aye, a fair question that needs answering," said Mr. King.

"I wear this coat," replied Boig, "because I was conscripted into Claverhouse's ranks."

"Conscripted!" said Sandy M'Kethe. "Ye were made to serve against yer will?"

"Aye, and against my mother's will, if not my father's. My mother did her best to raise me to fix my hope on King Jesus, the Redeemer and only Head of his Kirk."

"Likely tale," snorted Balfour. "Corporal, is it? How a corporal if ye were conscripted?"

"This, too, needs answering," said Mr. King.

"My father's an officer in the king's garrison at Edinburgh," said Boig. "I'm ashamed to say it. He saw to my being conscripted and to my promotion. Och, believe me or no, every hour of my service under Claverhouse has been a burden too great to bear."

"That explains, then," said Mr. King. "Why ye spoke as ye did during the battle."

"*During* the battle?" said Angus.

"Aye, during," said Mr. King, turning to Angus. "Boig here was one of the three Claverhouse left to guard us during the battle—and to slit our throats if things went against the Crown." He looked meaningfully at Angus. "He's the one, lad, that got away."

"Ye wouldnae hae done it, though?" said Angus.

"Nae," said Boig, shaking his head sadly. "Never."

"But ye did prime yer pistol," said Angus. "I saw ye do it."

Boig gave Angus a puzzled look. "Aye. I primed my pistol so as to stop my comrades if it came to that. Then the strangest thing happened."

"What was that?" asked Sandy M'Kethe.

"Ye saw it, Mr. King," said Boig, rubbing his chin in bewilderment. "Arrows they were. Arrows came from nowhere—or from everywhere. And my comrades fell dead."

"Aye, and what did ye do about it?" growled Balfour.

"I dropped my pistol and ran. Och, man, whoever was shooting those arrows—he doesnae miss."

"In the name of God," said Sandy M'Kethe firmly, "Boig lives."

25 FEASTING AT THE CASTLE

. . . I perceive the way to life lies here.
Come, pluck up heart, let's neither faint nor fear.
Better, though difficult, the right way to go,
Than wrong, though easy, where the end is woe.

John Bunyan

Bloody Clavers' favorites, Captain Blyth and Crauford, shot before his very eyes," said Sir Robert Hamilton, his eyes wide as he stood before the long oak table in the great hall of Loudoun Castle later that night. A great log fire burned brightly in the fireplace, and tallow candles flickered along the stone walls, casting a glow that made Angus wonder with longing at what he'd heard about English Christmas celebrations.

Lord and Lady Loudoun sat on either side of Hamilton as he told the tale. They had spread their table to celebrate the great rout of Claverhouse and the great victory for the men of the Covenant. After the fighting men had seen their children and families safely home, all were invited to Loudoun Castle for feasting and thanksgiving. And the Loudoun table would not disappoint. It was richly loaded with boar and pheasant, roasted venison and haggis, hard Bonnet cheese and soft Bonchester cheese, and golden shortbread and sweet Dundee cakes—and great heaping plates of Dutch chocolate.

Angus's mouth watered. Flinch bobbed back and forth on his shoulder, eyeing the nearest plate of chocolate.

"The terrified remains of his army," continued Hamilton, "pounded after Claverhouse, doing their best to keep up with their fleeing commander. They clattered down country lanes in wide-eyed panic, and through wee villages a perfect glaive of flight. And I've heard that Clavers never reined his horse 'til safe in the walls of Glasgow."

"O Christ, ye're our hiding place," said Mr. King, rising to his feet, his arms lifted heavenward. "Ye've protected us from trouble and surrounded us with songs of deliverance. Praise, praise and glory to ye, O Christ."

"Amen!" sounded from the hall like a thunderclap.

"I only regret that we didnae cut the monster down this day," this from John Burly Balfour. "The word was 'No quarters.' But we let the bloody man flee."

"And there were others," said John Nisbet. "Prisoners were taken—" Here he broke off and stared at the faces filling the hall. Many diverted their eyes from his fierce glare, and the room grew silent. "Prisoners taken when the word was to cut down all the enemy. God commanded the same of Joshua at Ai, and he cut the enemies of Israel all down, leaving them neither survivors nor fugitives. Later, God caused the sun to stand still until the nation avenged itself on its enemies, totally destroying the Amorites, leaving no survivors. But, alas, when God fought for us at Drumclog this day, we've gone and left half done."

"But is it the same for Claverhouse to say 'No quarters,'" said Sandy M'Kethe, "as it was for God—when his wrath was full—to order Israel to totally destroy the wicked Canaanites?"

"Aye," said Mr. King. "Surely ye're not putting Clavers' word on a level with God's, man?"

"Och, no. But, mark ye, we'll face Claverhouse again," said Nisbet. "And then we'll wish we'd cut him down. Aye, we will."

"Aye, he now has potent reason to recover himself," agreed William Cleland. "And crush us once and for all."

"But doesnae God call us in his Word," said Mr. King, "to love mercy? And even in the midst of a battle to defend the innocent, we may show mercy." He looked over at Angus and raised an eyebrow meaningfully as he spoke. "We donnae want to become vengeful like our enemy, now, do we?"

"But the confessed enemies of the Kirk," said Nisbet, "are to be exterminated without mercy, as the Lord commanded Moses in his Word. Read the eleventh of Joshua. It's all there, man."

"I ken it's there," said Mr. King. "But are we told to go and do likewise here in Scotland? Is that there, too?"

"If ever there has been wickedness since the days of Joshua," replied Nisbet, a tremor of emotion in his voice, "it is here in Scotland in the person of Clavers and his dragoons. Loyalty to Christ and the Kirk means vengeance on her enemies. And Clavers is her enemy."

"We've lost but one in the field," said Cleland, "and five since from their wounds, including, of this parish, Thomas Fleming, who lies in state in the good earl's study to be buried in the old Kirk yard on the morrow. More than forty of Clavers' men lie cold this night. We must be grateful, and we must avenge our losses."

"Brothers, brothers," interrupted the earl. "We have gathered here to celebrate the Lord's great mercy to us this day. Let us not taint our gratitude with quarrelling. Now, then, I propose we sing our thanksgiving to the Lord."

They rose, and with one voice sang:

. . . My table thou hast furnished
In presence of my foes;
My head thou dost with oil anoint,
And my cup overflows.

And they ate and drank until all were filled. In the warm glow of the victory at Drumclog, and in the delights of good fare enjoyed together around a generous table, differences were, for the moment, suspended if not forgotten.

More than once during the meal Angus grabbed Flinch by the beak and scolded him for leaping onto the table and tearing away at his father's venison. But, then, chocolate was served.

"King and Kirk!" screeched the bird, diving off Angus's shoulder toward the plate of chocolate.

Angus grabbed at Flinch's legs just in time to avoid disaster.

"Angus, I'm a-thinking Flinch lacks the refinement needed to feast at an earl's table," said his father. "Gather up yer fowl, and let's us go for a wee stroll about the garden."

It was a beautiful summer evening, and the earl joined them.

" 'Twas a great victory for the Kirk," said the earl as they walked along the crushed rock paths, the spicy scent of roses hanging in the evening air.

"Aye," said Angus.

"And Mr. King and the prisoners," continued the earl, "are most grateful for the part ye played in today's fighting. They owe ye their lives, Angus, as does Corporal Boig."

Angus's mind flickered back to the instant his arrow

struck the captain. Again he saw the dread and horror in the man's eyes as he groped at his neck and at the arrow. He saw him fall and lie still on the sod. An involuntary shudder ran down Angus's spine.

His father slipped his arm around Angus's shoulder. For a moment Angus longed to be a little boy again and curl up on his father's lap and go to sleep. They walked on in silence for several moments.

"But I'd like victory better," said Angus, at last, "if it were the final victory . . . and there was peace . . . and no more killing. I'd like that better."

"As would we all, lad," agreed the earl.

"But will it ever be?" asked Angus. The blood-pounding strain of that day suddenly descended on his young soul like a storm cloud. He felt very tired. "I fear we'll never have freedom to worship God—not here in Scotland."

"That remains hidden, lad," said his father, "in the mystery of God's all-merciful providence."

"But, Father, would it be a sin to flee far away," asked Angus, "far away from all this killing? And there live and work and worship in peace? Would it be a sin?"

"Angus, Angus," said the earl, reprovingly. "Here we've been granted by the Lord the greatest deliverance against his and our enemies, and ye're wanting to get on a ship and join the Puritans in America—I ken what ye're thinking. Be grateful for this great triumph, lad, and leave the rest to God."

"What ye're longing for, lad," said his father, "is heaven. Aye, ye might find more freedom for a time in other lands. But, I'm thinking, it'd only be for a time. Nae, lad. Fix yer hope on heaven, and be faithful to God's summons while abiding here in this our benighted Scotland."

They walked on in silence for a moment, their boots crunching rhythmically on the gravel path.

"But, will this victory—" asked Angus, when several moments had past, "—will Drumclog lead to more freedom, or to more woe?"

Angus's father did not immediately reply. He walked on in silence.

"It was a *great victory*, Angus," said the earl with mild irritation. "Be content!"

"I ken I ought to be more grateful," said Angus, studying the dim pathway at his feet. "But, do ye think we have them in check, then?" Angus managed a slight grin as he looked inquiringly up at the earl.

"Aye, in check," replied the earl. "In check," he repeated, in a tone full of considerably more finality than he felt.

Some of the men had lit a bonfire, and Angus watched the sparks fly upward as the wood burned and crackled, brilliantly illuminating the central turret of the castle against the night sky. Shadowy figures stood out in silhouette against the brightness.

"Ye ken chess, Angus," said the earl. "And though ye fought valiantly today, Angus, yer father and I ken more than ye of kings, of bishops, and bloody soldiers—the real ones."

"Aye," said Angus, waiting for the earl to finish.

"Och," blurted the earl. "I fear we'll have woes aplenty before we have Charles in checkmate." He kicked at the gravel with his boot. "And, thus, there will be much work for faithful and valiant men to do—men like ye, Angus."

"Aye," agreed Sandy M'Kethe, gripping his son's shoulder firmly. "Like ye, Angus."

Angus looked up at his father. The quavering

flames from the bonfire shimmered in the deep blue of his eyes. For a moment Angus felt sorry for King Charles and all his minions. If the king only knew his father, really knew him, Angus was certain the king would do anything to be his friend and not his enemy.

"Aye, lad," continued his father, in a tone full of that mysterious blending of strength and tenderness. "Duties are ours, Angus. And ye shall have duties enough in days ahead, I should think. But for now—and always—leave the events to God. Remember, my son, come wind, come weather, we're in King Jesus' hands, not in King Charles's."

A WORD ABOUT THE HISTORY AND CHARACTERS

The battle at Drumclog, and the events leading up to the battle, are real events that occurred at real places (see map) and involved real people who lived and died because of their loyalty to Christ's Crown and Covenant. Angus M'Kethe and his family, though fictional, authentically represent the faith and struggles of many during these trying years of persecution in Scotland. Listed below in alphabetical order are the names of historical figures that appear in the story.

Ayton, Andrew, of Inchdarnie
Balfour, John Burly
Blyth, Captain
Boig, John
Cameron, Richard
Campbell, John, Earl of Loudoun
Cargill, Donald
Cleland, William
Crauford, Captain
Crookshanks, John
Dingwall, William

Douglas, Thomas
Fleming, Thomas
Graham, John, of Claverhouse
Hackston, David
Hall, Henry, of Haugh-head
Hamilton, Sir Robert
King, John
Lauderdale, Chancellor
Lord of Torfoot
Nevay, John
Nisbet, John
Paton, Captain John
Paton, Matthew
Sharp, Archbishop
Sutherland, William
Turner, Sir James
Welsh, John (spelled *Welch* by some historians)
Wilkie, Thomas

GLOSSARY OF SCOTTISH TERMS

Aye: yes
Bairn: child
Bannock: flat oatmeal cake baked on a griddle
Bonnie: pretty
Brae: hillside
Breeks: loose trousers ending near the knee
Burn: stream
Claymore: great sword; in the seventeenth century the heavy Scottish sword with basket hilt
Cess: forced tax levied on Scottish nobles to maintain royal troops
Croft: small, low farmhouse
Daft limmer: crazy woman
Didnae: did not
Daft: silly
Dirk: a short straight dagger
Doesnae: does not
Donnae: do not
Ferm-toun: small cluster of homes away from an established village
Gang: gone

Glaive: halberd with a swordlike blade; used figuratively as "a glaive of light"

Glen: valley

Hae: have

Haggis: ground sheep organs and oatmeal boiled in sheep stomach

Hasnae: has not

Indulged: name for ministers who accepted the indulgence offered to Covenanting ministers in 1669. The Non-Indulged clergy saw the indulgence as a compromise with episcopacy.

Ken: know

Kent: knew

Lad: boy

Lass: girl

Loch: lake

Muckle: much

Nae: No or not

Non-compearance: failure to conform to Anglican worship

Och: expression of dismay, woe, or dismissal

Perfidious: treacherous

Plaid: long, cross-patterned, wool cloth worn over the shoulder

Sporran: leather pouch worn at the front of a kilt

Wee: little

Whig: derisive name for Covenanters. Possibly an acronym for **W**e **H**ope **I**n **G**od

TIMELINE OF SCOTTISH COVENANTING HISTORY

1603	James VI of Scotland becomes James I King of England
1610	Bishops appointed to rule in Presbyterian Scotland
1618	Five Articles of Perth: James I further imposes Anglican worship in Scotland
1625	Death of James I; Charles I crowned
1637	Rejection of Laud's Liturgy (Jenny Geddes heaves her stool in St. Giles)
1638	Signing the National Covenant at Greyfriars Abbey
1639	Bishop's Wars begin
1642	Civil War begins
1643	Westminster Assembly; Samuel Rutherford and Scottish commissioners to London
1643	Solemn League and Covenant signed (English Puritans and Scottish Presbyterians pledge their nations to Presbyterian uniformity in religion)
1651	Covenanters crown Charles Stuart; Oliver Cromwell defeats Scottish army
1660	Restoration of monarchy; King Charles II betrays the Covenant
1661	Anglican worship re-imposed

1662	Faithful ministers ejected from their pulpits; field preaching begins
1663	Persecution and plunder by James Turner begins with a vengeance
1666	Pentland Rising; Battle of Rullion Green
1669	Declaration of Indulgence, dividing Covenanters into "Indulged" and "Non-Indulged" clergy
1670	Attendance at field meetings made treasonable offense. Preaching at field meetings made punishable by death
1678	*Pilgrim's Progress* by John Bunyan published in England
1679	May 3, murder of Archbishop Sharp
1679	May 29, Rutherglen Declaration
1679	June 1, Covenanter victory over Claverhouse at Drumclog

ACKNOWLEDGMENTS

I am grateful for the helpful criticism of my proofreaders, Lorna Arnold and John Schrupp, and for the supply of books and critical information about Scottish Church history from The Rev. Dr. Robert S. Rayburn and from The Rev. Douglas Lamb of the Scottish Covenanters Memorials Association in Scotland. Special thanks to Gaelic-speaking The Rev. John McLeod, minister of the Church of Scotland at Loudoun Parish Church, Newmilns, Ayrshire, for his help with the Gaelic used in this book.

Douglas Bond, a high school history and English teacher, has done extensive research on Scottish history, and has traveled many times to Scotland. He is the author of *Duncan's War* and the *Mr. Pipes* series of children's books. Bond has earned an M.I.T. in education from St. Martin's College. He lives with his wife and five children in Washington state.

CROWN & COVENANT SERIES

Duncan's War (Book 1)
King's Arrow (Book 2)
Rebel's Keep (Book 3)
